The Red Tenant

Donovan M. Neal

Tornveil

For permission requests, write to the publisher, addressed "Attention: Permissions Coordinator," at the email below:

tornveil@donovanmneal.com

Ordering Information:

Quantity sales. Special discounts are available on quantity purchases by corporations, associations, and others. For details, contact the publisher at the email address above.

Orders by U.S. trade bookstores and wholesalers. Please contact Lightning Source: Tel: (615) 213-5815; fax: (615) 213-4725 or visit https://www.lightningsource.com/.

Printed in the United States of America

ISBN 979-8-9890821-3-1 (Print Version)

Contents

Dedication

Dedication

I dedicate this book to those who dare to dream and see it through to completion. May your imagination ever lead you to new realms.

Acknowledgments

Acknowledgments

To the Lord Jesus Christ, who loves me.

To my children: Candace, Christopher and Alexander–you can do great things!

To the authors, comic books artists, and writers who have come before, and who unknowingly have breathed on the embers of my imagination.

To all my beta readers and friends who shared both critiques and encouragement.

To my beloved wife Nettie, you are the color to my world.

May God truly bless you all.

Chapter One

Bon Voyage

The harbor at La Rochelle smelled of salt, rot and ambition.

Antoine de la Mothe Cadillac walked the quay in the pale morning light of late May, the cobblestones still slick from the previous night's rain, his boots finding the uneven stones with the practiced ease of a man who had crossed worse ground than this. Around him the port churned with its usual controlled chaos—barrels rolled and thumped against wooden pallets, ropes groaned under tension, gulls screamed overhead like things being slowly killed. The air tasted of fish and tar and the particular heaviness that preceded long ocean crossings, as if the sea itself were already pressing in.

La Vigilante sat low and dark in the water, her hull black with pitch, her rigging a tangle of lines against the colorless sky. She was a frigate of middling size and considerable age, and she wore both facts plainly. Her figurehead, some forgotten goddess, features worn smooth by years of Atlantic weather, stared ahead with the blank patience of the dead. Cadillac paused at the foot of the gangway and regarded her for a moment. She would carry him to Quebec, and from Quebec he would make himself into the continent's deep interior, to a place that existed so far only in royal dispatches and his own restless imagination. The orders from Minister Pontchartrain were folded inside his coat, pressed flat against his ribs, and he was aware of them the way a man is aware of a healing wound: constantly, and not without discomfort.

He produced the papers at the gangway. The captain of La Vigilante was a compact, weathered man named Moreau, with the unhurried manner of someone who had learned long ago that the sea could not be rushed and had extended this philosophy to all other matters. He examined Cadillac's credentials with the same deliberate calm he might apply to checking a weather glass, then handed them back with a nod.

"Welcome aboard Commandant." He turned. "Allow me—Renard, my first mate."

Renard was a broad-shouldered man one did not want to tussle, sharp-faced, with quick eyes that moved over Cadillac and arrived at some private conclusion before any words were exchanged. They shook hands. The three of them stood together at the rail above the gangway, and for a time there was little to say, so they said little, and watched instead the going ons of those that boarded and the men who prepped the Vigilante to get underway.

Various passengers heading to the new world settlers boarded. A husband and wife with several children in tow. A man, notary by trade. Blanchard was his name. He too passed the first mate and had his papers inspected. A cohort of French and Flemish men and a few women headed from Europe to start new lives.

He did not have to wait long before his own belongings came up the quay on a hired cart—two men laboring under the weight of his large trunk, a third managing the remaining cases. Cadillac watched them negotiate the gangway with the trunk and felt the familiar unease settle over him, the same unease that had accompanied every departure for as long as he could remember. It was not the crossing he dreaded. It was the cargo.

The trunk held the expected things. His uniforms, spare clothes, the three pistols wrapped in oilcloth, his grandfather's sword lay diagonally across the bottom, its scabbard worn but the blade sound. The cartographic roll with its instruments: sextant, calipers, dividers—the tools of a man who intended to put his name on unmapped places. The land grant documents, the ledgers, the contracts for the venture: the paper architecture of an enterprise that existed, as yet, only in the King's confidence and Cadillac's own will. He touched his coat pocket reflexively, feeling the slight weight of the silver compass there; his grandfather's, kept close always, a habit so old it had become instinct.

But it was not the trunk that occupied his thoughts. It was the smaller case, dark-stained leather, that one of the men was carrying under his arm with the careless ease of someone who did not know what he held. Cadillac watched it cross the gangway and resisted the urge to take it himself.

Inside, wrapped in cloth and nestled against one another like sleeping things, were the items his grandmother had pressed upon him the last time he saw her, three years before she died. He had thought her old and frightened then. He was less certain of that now. The dark wooden box with its brass latch and its carved symbols he could not read, not in any language he'd been taught. The three iron nails bound with red thread. The vial of salt. The bone-handled knife, its grip worn to the shape of a hand that was not his. And beneath all of it, folded small and creased to translucency, the paper in her handwriting. He did not need to open it. He had read it so many times that the words had ceased to feel like words and had become instead something closer to a pulse, a rhythm his mind returned to without his permission.

Never let the Rouge name you twice.

He had spent considerable effort, in the years since, constructing rational explanations for what she had meant. He had succeeded only in exhausting himself. The rosary was in there as well, smooth wooden beads, silver crucifix, his mother's hands around his when she gave it to him, and the prayer book wrapped in oilcloth, thin as whispers. He was not certain he believed in the protection they offered. He was entirely certain he was not willing to cross the Atlantic without them.

The case disappeared into the hold. Cadillac let out a breath he hadn't realized he'd been holding and turned back to Moreau and Renard.

"Quebec first," Moreau said, not really to anyone. "Then wherever the orders send you."

"Detroit," Cadillac said. The word felt strange in his mouth on French soil, in a French harbor, with France still visible in every direction. "We're to establish a fort. A settlement to control the straits between the upper lakes."

Renard made a sound that was not quite skepticism and not quite admiration. "A long way from Pontchartrain's office."

"Yes," Cadillac agreed. "That is rather the point." Renard chuckled in understanding.

Below them, the passengers continued to come in a slow, uneven procession up the gangplank. Cadillac observed them with the detached attention of a man accustomed to assessing strangers quickly and trusting his first impressions. Tradesmen with their tools crated and roped. Minor functionaries clutching documents. A priest who moved with the particular self-containment of someone who had made peace with wherever God chose to send him. Families, some of them, women with children pressed close, husbands carrying what remained of everything they owned. Their faces were uniformly the same: that mixture of resolution and barely suppressed dread that belonged to people who had committed themselves to something too large to fully comprehend.

Then a woman in a dark traveling cloak made her way up the gangplank, one hand gripping the rope rail, the other holding fast to the wrist of a small girl, eight years old, perhaps, with her mother's careful eyes and her own barely contained energy. The child looked up at the ship as she climbed, head tipping back, taking in the masts and the rigging and the gray sky beyond with an expression of uncomplicated wonder.

"Her husband's already gone ahead," Renard said quietly beside him, as if reading Cadillac's attention. "Crossed the Atlantic last autumn. She's been waiting out the winter."

Cadillac nodded but said nothing. He watched the woman reach the deck, watched her take in the confined space of the ship with a composed expression that cost her something to maintain. She was younger than he'd first thought. The child tugged at her hand, already straining toward the rail, toward the water, toward whatever came next.

He descended to the deck as the procession continued, exchanging a few final words with Moreau about the morning's departure, and it was then—just as he turned toward the gangway, that the little girl broke from her mother's side and raced towards him.

She held out a small fist, opening it to reveal a scrap of bright red ribbon, no wider than two fingers, tied in a clumsy bow. "For luck, Monsieur Cadillac," she said in a whisper, eyes wide and earnest. "So, the sea stays kind, and we all arrive safe."

Cadillac's gloved hand extended automatically: then froze. The ribbon caught the weak sunlight, a vivid crimson slash against the drab wood and canvas around them. Red. Too red with the design of an imp's face sewn into the fabric. Like the face in the old tales his grandmother whispered on winter nights: the face of the Nain Rouge, the red dwarf who danced on the graves of the arrogant, eyes like coals, grinning with teeth like broken glass. A child's gift, innocent as spring, but the color and face struck him like a slap. His stomach twisted; for an instant he saw not a ribbon but a bloodied scrap, or the gleam of those legendary eyes watching from somewhere deep in the hold, on the dark wooden box that sat latched and waiting, a family heirloom carved with symbols no one had ever translated for him.

He recoiled half a step before catching himself and forced a thin smile. "Merci, petite," he managed, his voice rougher than intended. He took it gingerly, as if it might burn, and tucked it into his cuff without looking at it again. The girl beamed, curtsied awkwardly, and scampered back to her mother.

He had taken no more than three steps up the gangplank when a sharp crack split the gray air above him, loud enough that several passengers flinched and ducked. A block and tackle had torn free from the main yard, and the heavy iron-fitted pulley swung in a vicious arc on its rope, trailing loose cordage that lashed across the deck and sent two deckhands scrambling. The freed rope end whipped against the rail hard enough to splinter wood, and the whole arrangement swayed and creaked overhead like a pendulum finding its rhythm.

"Get that line—now!" yelled Moreau. "Duplessis, the yard, move!" Captain Moreau's voice cut across the harbor noise, sharp and absolute. He was already moving, shouldering past the frozen passengers, eyes up. The men responded instantly, swarming the rigging, calling back and forth as they worked to haul the swinging block under control. It took longer than it should have. The pulley turned slowly at the end of its rope, iron catching the pale light, until at last Seaman Duplessis got a hand on the line and brought it to heel.

Cadillac stood beneath it, jaw set, watching the men re-secure the tackle with quick, chastened hands. Around him the passengers had gone very quiet. The little girl had buried her face back in her mother's skirts.

"Knot work," he said to no one in particular, his voice flat. "We haven't even left the harbor."

He turned and walked aboard without looking at the ribbon in his cuff.

Chapter Two

The Compass

For three days the Vigilante sailed the ocean. And Cadillac had settled into the routine that was his custom when embarked at sea.

On this fourth morning's journey, the rhythm was now comfortable, like worn leather. A day of journaling and reviewing the many issues given by the king to authorize his journey. The review of reports by the ship's doctor on his settler's health. He studied the names of those who would eventually sail with him on the expedition to the location the scouts had gained through the travels through the wilderness. Intelligence that a patch existed south along a river and that he should attempt his settlement there. He looked at the survey map, and his compass gleamed on his desk.

The silver compass had belonged to Antoine's grandfather, and before that to someone whose name had been lost to time and poor record-keeping, and the particular carelessness with which the de la Mothe family had always treated its own history. It was a beautiful instrument, or had been at one time. The case was engraved with a vine pattern worn nearly smooth by decades of thumbs; the needle balanced on a pivot so fine it trembled at the slightest provocation, sensitive as a sick man's pulse. Antoine had carried it since he was nineteen years old. He knew its habits the way one knows the habits of a horse ridden for years, the small quirks and tendencies that added up to a kind of personality.

Which was how he noticed, on the fourth morning out from La Rochelle, that it was wrong.

Not dramatically wrong. Not the kind of wrong that would make a man shout for the helmsman or drag out the charts. Two degrees, maybe two and a half, the needle sitting just slightly east of where it ought to be sitting given the sun's position and the wind and Antoine's eleven years of accumulated knowledge about where north actually was. He stood at the starboard rail in the early morning light and turned the compass in his hand and looked at it as you look at a friend who has just said something slightly odd at a dinner party, uncertain whether you heard correctly, uncertain whether it matters.

He tapped the glass. The needle trembled and settled back to the same wrong position.

He put the compass away and told himself it was the case. Silver warped. Everyone knew that. He had been meaning to have the instrument recalibrated for two years and had never gotten around to it, and this was simply the consequence of that negligence catching up with him at an inconvenient moment. Nothing more.

Still, he thought about it through the morning watch. Cadillac walked to see the cabin, fiddling with his compass in his pocket. He knocked on the door. "Enter," grumbled the grizzled man.

Captain Moreau was hovering over his table; his charts spread and weighted against the Atlantic wind that found its way through every gap in the ship's structure, when Antoine approached him. He felt faintly ridiculous doing it. He was a man who had commanded settlements, who had stood in the offices of ministers and argued policy with men who had the King's ear. He should not be approaching a ship's captain with his grandfather's compass like a schoolboy with a broken toy.

"A moment?" he said.

Moreau looked up. He was a compact man, dark-complexioned from his many years at sea, with the kind of face that had been weathered past the point of showing age, he could have been forty-five or sixty and it would have made no difference. His eyes were the particular shade of gray that belonged to men who had spent their lives looking at water.

"My compass," Antoine said, and produced it for the captain's inspection. "I think the case may have warped. The needle is sitting off." He held it out, feeling the slight heat of embarrassment in his face. "Two degrees, perhaps. I wondered if you might..."

Moreau took the compass without comment and looked at it, eying the device from every angle then he set it on the chart table and produced his own brass instrument from his coat pocket, larger, less elegant, the kind of tool that had been bought for utility rather than sentiment. He then set them side by side.

Antoine's compass: two degrees east of north.

Moreau's compass: true.

"Silver cases warp," Moreau said, not unkindly. He handed the instrument back. "The metal moves with temperature and humidity. Atlantic crossings are hard on fine instruments. Have it recalibrated when you reach Quebec." He paused. "I wouldn't navigate by it."

"No," Antoine agreed. "Of course not. Thank you."

He put the compass away. "Is there anything else, Commandant? I am busy reviewing our position."

"No, Captain. Thank you for your time." Moreau returned to his charts, and that was the end of it.

Except.

Antoine was a man who noticed things. He had built a career on noticing things, gambling also told you much about whether men lied. All men gave tells body language that belied their inner thoughts. I careful observer could home in on the tension in a man's jaw that told you he was lying. Observation could reveal the way a treeline changed that told you a river was coming, or the slight discrepancies between what a map said versus what the ground spoke. All tells of man or nature that could mean the difference between a successful expedition and a column of men dying of thirst in the wrong valley. Noticing was not a skill he had cultivated so much as a reflex he had been born with, and he had long since stopped being able to turn it off.

So, that evening he noticed what Moreau's face did.

It was late, the eight o'clock watch had just rung, and most of the passengers had gone below, and the deck had settled into the particular quiet that belonged to an Atlantic crossing at night, when the ship felt less like a vessel and more like a small lit room suspended in an enormous darkness. Moreau was still at his cabin's stern table, finishing his calculations by lantern light. Antoine passed behind him on the way to his cabin when he glanced over, more out of habit than intention.

It was then that he saw Moreau staring at his compass.

However, Antoine's attention was arrested not on his action but his expression. Moreau was a man whose face, in Antoine's four days of observation, had communicated a range of emotions roughly bounded by faint satisfaction and mild displeasure and the surety of command. He was not a demonstrative man, save to communicate authority. The kind of captain who delivered bad news in the same tone he delivered good news and let the facts speak for themselves.

But his face now showed something Antoine had not seen before. It was still, in the particular way that a face stills when the brain behind it has received information it was not expecting and is taking a moment to decide what to do with that information. It was the stillness of a man who had checked his footing and found the ground slightly wrong, not collapsed, not obviously dangerous, but wrong. Not where it was a moment ago.

Moreau tapped the compass glass with one finger. Set it down. Picked it up. Looked at it again.

Antoine continued walking. His pace was deliberate and steady. He did not look back.

He walked back to his cabin and sat on his cot in the dark for a while without lighting the lantern. The ship moved around him, the familiar Atlantic rhythm, caused the ship to bellow the groan of timber and the indistinct sound of water against the hull that had become, in four days, as unremarkable as breathing. His grandfather's compass was in his coat pocket. He took it out and turned it in his fingers in the dark, feeling the engraved vines, the worn patches where the engraving had been rubbed smooth.

Two degrees off. Silver cases warp, he told himself.

He put it away.

* * *

Later during the night, he got up from his cot and lit the lantern, and opened his logbook to that evening's entry. Penning the date, position, wind speed, and ship's heading. He wrote two lines about the survey he'd reviewed earlier that morning. He sat for a moment with the pen in his hand; the nib drying.

Then he wrote: Grandfather's compass reading 2° E of true. Case may be warped. Captain's instrument verified true at 14:00 hours.

He stared at what he wrote for a moment.

Then he wrote: Captain's instrument re-examined by captain at approximately 20:00 hours. His expression suggested an anomalous reading. He said nothing.

He looked at that, too.

Then he closed the logbook and put it away and blew out the lantern and lay on his cot with his coat pulled over him and his grandfather's compass in his hand, the worn metal case just slightly cool against his palm similar to how metal holds the cold, and he looked at the dark ceiling and listened to the ship, and tried to think of nothing in particular, and mostly succeeded as he drifted to sleep.

* * *

The morning's routine meeting with the senior staff was not amiss.

The captain did not mention his compass at breakfast, and Antoine did not ask.

And the ship continued on its heading.

Above them, the Atlantic sky was that particular hard blue of summer, cloudless and immense and entirely indifferent, and the wind was fair, and by every visible measure the morning was unremarkable. Twenty-seven men going about the business of keeping a 300-ton vessel pointed in the right direction, and whatever was in Moreau's pocket sitting slightly wrong against his thigh, and whatever was in Antoine's fist sitting slightly wrong against his palm, and neither man said anything about it to the other because what was there to say, really.

Silver cases warp.

Of course, they do.

Go back to work.

Chapter Three

Some things won't stay shut.

The second watch bell had just rung when the knock came.

Antoine had been asleep for perhaps two hours, which on a ship seven days out from La Rochelle meant he had been asleep for precisely as long as the Atlantic would allow before some new misery presented itself. He lay in the dark for a moment after the knock, cataloging his body as has woken suddenly, ribs intact, head clear enough, the low persistent ache in his lower back that had been with him since Biscay showing no signs of improvement or departure. Then he pulled on his coat and opened the door.

One of Moreau's junior sailors stood in the passage, a boy of perhaps sixteen with a lantern and the expression of someone who had drawn the short straw.

"The captain's apologies, Monsieur Cadillac. He asked if you would come to his quarters."

Moreau's quarters were like his own, at the stern, above his own, and were small but private, smelling of tobacco and the particular concentrated brine that gathered in enclosed spaces on long crossings.

The captain was seated at his chart table in his shirtsleeves, which Antoine had not seen before and found faintly alarming in the way that minor violations of a careful man's habits are always alarming. He had not been sleeping. There were no charts open in front of him.

He looked up when Antoine entered, and his expression expressed a man exercising patience at some cost to himself.

"Your trunk," Moreau said.

Antoine waited.

"It bangs," Moreau said. "Every time we take a swell, and we have been taking swells since Ushant, as you may have noticed, something inside it strikes the latch. My cabin is directly above your berth." He paused. "I have not slept since Ushant."

Antoine opened his mouth to say something and then closed it again because there was nothing useful to say. Moreau was not a man who exaggerated, and La Rochelle had been a week ago.

"I apologize," Antoine said. "I'll see to it tonight."

"Yes," Moreau agreed. "You will."

* * *

The berth Antoine had been assigned was a narrow space partitioned from the common quarters by a canvas curtain, private by the standards of the crossing, which meant only that the other passengers could hear him breathe rather than watch him do it. His large trunk sat against the forward wall, secured with the rope lashing he'd put on it himself in La Rochelle, the knots tight enough that he'd had to use a belaying pin to work them free twice already when he needed something from inside.

He crouched in front of it with the lantern and undid the lashing and opened the lid.

Everything was as he had packed it. The cartographic roll in its leather sleeve, tight and dry. The ledger and the contracts lay flat against the base, wrapped in oilcloth. Two changes of clothes folded with the same military precision his mother had drilled into him at an age when he would rather have been outside. The three pistols wrapped separately, each in its own cloth. His grandfather's sword in its scabbard along the right interior wall. The prayer book and the rosary nested together in the corner.

And the grandmother's box, sitting where he'd put it, in the left-front quadrant of the trunk's interior, its brass latch closed. He pressed his thumb against the latch. It was firm.

He studied the interior of the trunk for some time, looking for the culprit. Nothing was loose. Nothing was positioned in a way that would let it swing or shift against the latch with the ship's movement. He lifted the cartographic roll and set it aside. He moved the ledger. He pressed down on the clothes to see if they had settled in a way that created any gaps.

Nothing. Everything was tight, everything was secured, everything was exactly where it should be in a trunk that had apparently been assaulting the captain's sleep for four days and showed no signs of how.

He repacked everything with the methodical care of a man who has learned that carelessness costs more than it saves. He added a folded shirt between the grandmother's box and the trunk's left wall. He added a rolled pair of stockings between the box and the cartographic instruments. He pressed everything down and tested the gaps with his fingers, and found none. Then he closed the lid and threaded a leather cord through the latch and tied it off with a knot that would have satisfied a bosun's inspection.

He sat back on his heels and looked at the trunk.

The ship moved through a long swell, rising and dropping in that slow Atlantic rhythm that stopped feeling like motion after the third day and became instead just the texture of the world, much like the ground breathed. The trunk sat against the wall and was silent and still.

"There," Antoine said to no one.

Then he allowed himself to drift off to sleep.

* * *

In the morning, the leather cord was on the floor.

He almost stepped on it getting up, the loop of it catching his eye in the gray early light coming through the porthole. He stood looking at it for a moment, the cord on the floor, before he looked at the trunk and saw the latch standing open.

He crouched down. The knot he had tied, a bowline, the same knot he had tied ten thousand times in twenty years at sea, a knot that did not come undone without assistance, was intact. The cord had not slipped. It had not worked loose in the night. It was a complete, sound bowline sitting on the floor, which meant the latch had passed through it somehow, or the cord had passed over the latch, either of which required a sequence of events for which Antoine could not construct a satisfying explanation for.

He opened the trunk.

Everything was as he had repacked it. The instruments, the documents, the clothes. The pistols. The sword. The prayer book. He moved his eyes methodically across the interior as he would move his eyes across a manifest, checking each item against the record in his memory.

The grandmother's box was in its place. He looked at its brass clasp for a long time. He was nearly certain, not entirely certain, but nearly, that he had pressed the clasp closed before tying the cord. He had the memory of doing it, the small click of the mechanism seating, though he acknowledged to himself that memories of routine actions in lamplight at midnight were not the most reliable class of evidence. Nearly certain was not entirely certain.

The clasp was standing upright. Open, or rather unclosed, the small, curved arm of it raised at an angle that was either the position of a clasp that had been closed and then opened or a clasp that had never been fully closed in the first place, and Antoine could not say which with any confidence he trusted.

He pressed it closed. He heard it click.

He repacked the trunk, added more cloth around the box, and closed the lid. He did not tie the cord again—the cord had clearly accomplished nothing, and he had no interest in finding it on the floor a second morning in a row. He closed the latch, pressed it to make certain it had been seated, and stood up.

He did not open his grandmother's box. He had reasons for this that he did not examine too carefully, the same way he had reasons for not opening his mother's letter, the same way a man has reasons for not pressing on a bruise that he suspects is worse than it looks. The box had been his grandmother's, and before that it had been someone else's, and the things inside it belonged to a conversation about his family that he had been postponing since before he left France. He was not ready for that conversation.

He was not ready.

He picked up the leather cord from the floor and coiled it, and put it in his coat pocket, and went up to breakfast.

* * *

The banging had started again sometime after the first watch bell.

Antoine knew this not because he heard it, his berth was below Moreau's quarters, and the sound traveled up through the planking in a way that made it inaudible to the man causing it and perfectly audible to the man beneath, but because of how Moreau looked at him the following morning.

He was at the mainmast checking the rigging schedule with Renard when he felt it, that specific quality of attention that meant someone was watching him with purpose. He turned. Moreau was standing at the entrance to the stern passage, twenty feet away, and he was not moving toward Antoine and he was not moving away, just standing there with his arms at his sides and his gray eyes level and steady, and Antoine understood the message with the clarity of a man who has received similar messages from similar men over the course of a long military career.

Come here.

He said something to Renard; but he didn't remember afterward what it was, something reasonable, something that covered his departure, and walked to where Moreau was standing. The captain turned without speaking and led him around the stern housing to the lee side, out of the wind, out of the main traffic on the deck. It was a narrow space, the rail on one side and the housing wall on the other, and it afforded the particular privacy of a ship at sea, which was not real privacy but was the closest approximation available: no one could hear them over the wind and the working sounds of the vessel, but anyone who looked would see two men in conversation, which was fine. Two men in conversation were not remarkable. Two men in conversation on the lee side of the stern housing, with the captain's face doing what Moreau's face was currently doing, was more remarkable, but there was nothing to be done about that.

Moreau stopped and turned to face him.

"It started again," he said. "After the second bell. It went until the fourth."

Antoine opened his mouth.

"I tied a cord through the latch," he said. "A bowline. I tied it myself."

"I know what a bowline is," Moreau said. "The cord did not appear to help."

"I don't understand what's shifting. I checked everything. I packed everything tight, I..."

"Monsieur Cadillac." Moreau's voice was not loud. It was never loud. It had the quality of a voice that had learned long ago that volume was for men who weren't being listened to, and Moreau was always listened to. "I am not here to discuss the packing. I am here because if you cannot secure your trunk, I will secure it for you, and you will not enjoy my method. Or..." a slight pause, the weight of which Antoine felt in his chest, "...I will have it moved to the forward hold, where it can bang against whatever it likes without disturbing the navigation of this vessel."

"The hold," Antoine said, and heard something in his own voice that he didn't entirely like, a tightness that gave away more than he intended.

Moreau heard it too. His eyes moved over Antoine's face with the evaluating quality of a man who has learned to read weather in things other than clouds.

"The hold," he confirmed. "It is a reasonable solution. It is where cargo belongs."

"My instruments are in that trunk. My commission documents. I need access..."

"You may access it during daylight hours under the watch's supervision." Moreau said this how he said everything, as if it were already decided, as if the conversation was less a negotiation than a notification. "Or you secure it tonight. Those are the options available to you."

From around the corner of the housing, not ten feet away from where the mainmast lines ran aft, Antoine heard a voice. Two sailors, he recognized one as Laurent, the older Norman who worked the dawn watch, the other he didn't know by name, engaged in the low-register conversation of men who are trying to seem like they are not listening while demonstrably listening.

"...at least three nights now," Laurent was said. "I thought it was the water casks at first. Something's loose in the hold."

"Not the hold," the other man said. "It's coming from above. From the passenger berths."

"I haven't slept a full watch in..."

"I know. Gauthier thought it was rats. He set a trap." A pause. "No rats."

Moreau had not turned toward the voices. He was still looking at Antoine. His expression did not change, but something in it deepened slightly, an additional layer of meaning added to what was already there.

“Do you hear that?” said Moreau.

“This is not only my problem.”

“No, but it is becoming *their* problem, and when things become their problem, they stop being polite about it in the way that I am *currently* being polite about it.”

Antoine looked at the captain and then looked at the two sailors, who had not quite managed to become invisible despite their best efforts. Laurent was coiling a line with the focused intensity of a man who is definitely not eavesdropping. The other man was looking at the water with great interest.

"A crew that doesn't sleep," Moreau said quietly, for Antoine's ears only, "is a crew that makes mistakes. A crew that makes mistakes on a three-hundred-ton vessel in the North Atlantic is a crew that kills people." He let that sit for a moment. "It is also a crew that looks for explanations. For causes. For someone... responsible." Another pause. "You understand me?"

Antoine understood him. He understood him with a clarity that had nothing to do with the words being spoken and everything to do with the eleven days he had already spent watching this particular community of men compact itself under pressure, watching the fault lines form and the resentments accumulate and the fear go looking for places to bed itself. A crew that wasn't sleeping was a crew that was already irritable, already primed, already doing the arithmetic of blame.

And he was the passenger with the noisy trunk.

"I'll fix it tonight," Antoine said.

"Yes," Moreau said. "You will."

He turned and walked around the housing and was gone, in the manner Moreau moved through all conversations, as if the matter were concluded the moment he decided it was concluded, and the other party's relationship to that conclusion was their own affair.

Antoine stayed where he was for a moment. Around the corner, he heard Laurent say something in a lower voice, and the other man laugh, the short, humorless laugh of someone who is tired and not amused. Then their voices moved away forward with the purposeful quality of men who had decided they were not where they were.

The wind came off the cold water and smelled of rain that hadn't arrived yet. Antoine gripped the rail and looked at the gray Atlantic and thought about the trunk. About the cord, which had been tied and found on the floor. About the grandmother's box with its brass clasp standing open in the morning light. About what was inside the box that he had not yet let himself look at, because looking at it would mean something he was not prepared to mean yet.

He thought about what Moreau had said.

"They look for causes. For someone responsible."

He thought about Gervais, down in the eating quarters, already laying the groundwork for exactly that kind of arithmetic. He thought about how the men's eyes moved when he passed them in the passages, that slight flicker that meant he was being evaluated and the evaluation was not entirely favorable. He thought about how quickly a collection of frightened people could agree on a story, and how much easier it was to agree on a story than to tolerate the absence of one.

He needed to fix the trunk. He knew this.

He also knew, and this was the part he was having more difficulty with, that he did not know how to fix the trunk. He had repacked it. He had tied it. He had checked it with his own hands in lamplight and found nothing loose, nothing that could be shifting in the manner it would need to shift to produce what Moreau was describing. Three nights of banging, stopping and starting, resuming after the second bell as if something had been waiting for the ship to quiet before beginning again.

Not something, he told himself. Not something. A loose instrument, a document that had worked itself into a position where it could move, the sea itself working on a latch mechanism that was older than it should have been. These were explanations. These were the kinds of explanations that a rational man in the year seventeen hundred produced when confronted with phenomena he could not immediately account for. He was a rational man. He had a royal commission.

He pushed off the rail and went below.

In his berth, he crouched in front of the trunk and opened it and removed everything. Every document, every instrument, every article of clothing. He laid them on the cot behind him in careful sequence. He turned the trunk upside down and checked the interior walls for any loose piece of wood that could be rattling against the frame. He turned it right-side up and examined the latch mechanism, found the pivot pin that held it, and tested it for play. There was play, a millimeter, perhaps less, the kind of wear that came with age, but not enough to explain anything.

He put everything back. Carefully. Precisely. Clothing flat, instruments wrapped and wedged, documents weighted and layered. The grandmother's box went in last, in the center of the left-front quadrant where he had put it before, and he pressed the clasp closed with his thumb and held it for three full seconds and felt it seated, felt the mechanism catch.

He closed the lid and engaged the latch.

He sat back on his heels and looked at the trunk and said nothing, because there was nothing to say to a trunk, and he was a rational man.

Then he went up to his cot and lay down and stared at the canvas ceiling and listened.

He was not sure how long he lay there. Long enough for the ship to settle into its night rhythms, for the voices above to thin out and the foot traffic on the deck to slow. The Atlantic moved under them with its long patient swells. The timbers spoke their usual language of stress and accommodation.

Silence from the trunk.

He was most of the way to sleep when he heard it.

Not a bang. Not the dramatic percussion that Moreau had described. Just a sound, small and precise, the sound of a brass clasp disengaging. A small mechanical click in the dark of his berth, as clear as a finger-snap, as deliberate as a question.

He did not get up.

He lay still and listened to the dark. After a while, he heard or thought he heard — and he was a rational man, and the ship made many sounds, and exhaustion played tricks — something like the sound of paper rustling. The dry whisper of old paper unfolding in a closed space.

Then nothing.

He lay there until the first watch bell rang, and then he got up in the dark, lit the lantern, and opened the trunk. The grandmother's box was open. The clasp was standing upright. Inside, everything was as if he had not looked at it, the iron nails and the vial and the knife and the folded paper in his grandmother's hand.

He closed the box. He latched it. He closed the trunk.

He sat on the edge of his cot with the lantern burning until morning came, and he did not sleep, and he did not open the box, and he did not think about what it meant that the box seemed to want to be opened.

He was not ready.

Below him, through the planking, Moreau's quarters were silent.

The banging did not resume that night.

Chapter Four

Robin the Rouge-gorge

Day ten on the Atlantic and the sky was the color of old pewter, the kind of sky that couldn't decide whether it wanted to rain and had been putting off the decision for hours. The ship moved through low swells with the slow patience of something that had been making this crossing longer than any man aboard had been alive, and Antoine was at the starboard rail doing what he had found himself doing with increasing frequency in the last three days: standing still and looking at the water and trying to feel like a man who had everything under control.

He heard her before he saw her. Small feet on the deck planking, that particular light quick sound that belonged only to children, who had not yet learned to move through the world with the flat-footed resignation of adults.

Marguerite stopped beside him at the rail. She came up to approximately his elbow. She put her hands on the rail, mimicking how he had his hands on the rail, and looked out at the water with an expression of serious consideration, as if she were evaluating it.

"Monsieur Cadillac," she said.

"Mademoiselle," he said.

They stood together for a moment in what was, Antoine realized, a surprisingly companionable silence for a man in his late thirties and a child of eight who had spoken perhaps forty words to each other total.

"Are you still wearing the ribbon?" she asked.

He had, in fact, transferred it from his cuff to the inner pocket of his coat on day three, unwilling to throw it away and equally unwilling to examine why. He patted the pocket now, felt the small lump of it.

"I am," he said.

She nodded, satisfied. "Good. It's important."

He looked down at her. In the gray morning light, she looked tiny and very certain, the way children look when they have been told something by an adult they trust completely and have not yet developed the machinery to doubt it. Her dark hair was braided back, and she was missing a front tooth, which gave her smile, when it came, a gap-toothed quality that made her look simultaneously younger and older than eight.

"How are you finding the crossing?" He asked, because he was a man who asked questions, it was the habit of his life, and because he was curious about this child in a way he couldn't entirely account for.

"It's soaked," she said, with the gravity of a mariner reporting conditions. "And it smells. Maman says I am not to complain."

"Your mother is wise."

"She says that, too." A pause. "My friend has been keeping me company. And Maman, of course."

Antoine looked at the water. "Your friend," he said carefully. "From the ship?"

"No," Marguerite said. "My new friend. The one I made after we left." She said it simply, just as children report facts that appear to them as self-evident. "He told me not to worry about what will happen...when people die." She considered this. "He said it isn't as bad as it looks. And that he would keep me safe." Another pause, almost an afterthought: "He said he would keep you safe too, Monsieur Cadillac. He also hoped you got a good night's sleep last night. I thought you would want to know."

The rail was solid under Antoine's hands. The ship was solid under his feet. The Atlantic was doing nothing unusual in any direction he could see. But at that moment. He froze. His heart skipped a beat. He looked at the child as if she was a contagion. And for a moment fear gripped him. He quickly recovered and replied.

"That's very kind, and my sleep was...uneventful" he said, and was pleased that his voice came out how it came out, which was steady and warm and gave away nothing of the cold that had started somewhere behind his sternum and was working its way outward. "Good! Robin hoped so. He doesn't like the captain. Doesn't like how he speaks to you."

"Marguerite."

The mother appeared from the hatchway with the slightly breathless quality of a woman who has learned that her child can cover ground faster than should be physically possible. She was a handsome woman in her thirties, tired in the way of someone who had been traveling alone with a small child for almost two weeks and had not slept as much as she would have liked. Her name was Céleste, and she was going to meet her husband in Quebec, a fact Antoine knew because Renard had told him in his matter-of-fact manner, as Renard knew everything about everyone on the ship within approximately forty-eight hours of departure.

"I'm sorry, Commandant," she said, taking Marguerite by the shoulder with the practiced grip of a mother who has had this conversation before. "She wanders. And she talks..." a slight tightening around the eyes "...about her friend."

"It's no trouble," Antoine said.

"She has an imagination," Céleste said, which was the particular tone of voice that meant *'please do not take anything my child says seriously'* and also *'I am slightly worried about this myself, but I am not going to say so to a stranger.'* "Since we boarded, she's been talking to herself incessantly. She has never had an imaginary friend before."

Antoine cracked a half smile and replied, "Children find ways to manage long journeys," he said.

Céleste's smile was grateful and did not reach her eyes. "Yes. Of course." She steered Marguerite toward the hatch. The girl went without resistance but looked back over her shoulder at Antoine as she went, and her expression was the one he was coming to recognize, that steady, patient look, like someone waiting for a slow student to arrive at an answer the teacher has known for some time.

Antoine stayed at the rail and watched the water for a while after they had gone below.

He said he would keep you safe, too. Robin doesn't like the captain. Doesn't like the way he speaks to you.

He put his hand in his coat pocket and felt the ribbon there, a small scrap of red silk, and after a moment he took his shaking hand back out and went to find something useful to do.

***

Renard came to him on the evening of the twelfth day.

He came just as men come when they want to report something they are not sure is worth reporting, which is sideways, with preamble, working up to the actual subject through a series of related topics that allowed for a dignified retreat if the listener's expression suggested he was going to be dismissive. He talked about the rations first, and then about Van der Meer's ongoing grievance with Dubois, and then about the port-side rigging that wanted attention, and Antoine waited because he had been a commander long enough to know that the real subject was coming.

"The little girl," Renard said finally. "The passenger. The one with the braid."

Marguerite," Antoine said.

"I saw her this evening. On the forecastle." Renard was a large man, weathered and practical, with the kind of face that had been resolving problems at sea for thirty years without losing sleep over any of them. He was not comfortable right now. "At dusk. Standing at the rail, talking."

"Talking?"

"I thought she was with her mother. So, I didn't...I just walked past, you know how you do. But then I looked back." He stopped.

"And?" Antoine said.

"She was alone." He said it flat, like a man laying evidence on a table. "No one near her. I went back and checked...I walked the forecastle, and there was no one else there. She was talking to the rail. Or to the water. Or to..." He stopped again. "She wasn't frightened," he said. "That's the thing. She was... he searched for the word ...pleased. Like she was having a pleasant conversation."

Antoine looked at him. "What was she saying?"

"I couldn't make it out. The wind." Renard's enormous hands moved slightly at his sides, a gesture that belonged to a man who wanted to cross himself and was not sure how it would be received. "I've got daughters, Commandant. I know what it looks like when a child is talking to herself because she's lonely or she's playing. This wasn't that."

After Renard had gone, Antoine stood in the passage and thought about what it meant to take a thing seriously without appearing to take it seriously, and decided he had enough practice with the distinction to manage it.

***

He found Céleste the next morning at breakfast, eating alone while Marguerite slept, "she sleeps so well now", the mother said, with that same slightly bewildered gratitude. "Better than she has in months, honestly. Better than she sleeps at home." Antoine asked if the child had seemed troubled at all, unhappy, any bad dreams. Céleste shook her head. "None," she said. Whatever the crossing had done to the adults aboard, and it had done something to all of them, the cumulative weight of days with no land and shrinking provisions and the particular claustrophobia of community without escape, had apparently agreed with Marguerite.

"She has always been a serious child," Céleste said. "Since she was very small. She doesn't make friends easily. She's..." she considered, "...watchful. Her father says she thinks too much." A small, fond smile. "But she's been happy on this ship. Happier than I expected."

Antoine smiled, thanked her, and went about his day.

He watched Marguerite at the midday meal. She ate her salt pork and hardtack with the focused efficiency of a child who had learned that complaining about food produced no useful results. She talked to her mother about things she had seen through the porthole. She did not fidget or whine or any of the things that children on long sea crossings usually did, and Antoine had been on enough crossings to know what children on them usually did.

Twice she looked at him. Not the casual glance of a child who had noticed an adult nearby—something steadier, more considered. The second time, he held her gaze, and she held his back for three full seconds before returning to her food.

He did not know what to make of her. He knew he did not like the name. Marguerite. His grandmother's name, sitting in the mouth of an eight-year-old girl on a ship in the middle of the Atlantic, and he was not superstitious, he was a man of the new century, a man of science and reason and royal commission, and the fact that the name bothered him was simply evidence of the effect that ocean crossings had on the rational mind when the rational mind was given too little to do and too much time to do it in.

He was nearly convinced of this. Almost.

* * *

On the fourteenth day, he sat beside her.

He did it at the midday meal, sliding onto the bench across from her while her mother was fetching their bowls, casual enough that it wouldn't alarm anyone. Marguerite looked up at him with that expression—waiting, patient, like she had been expecting him to come around to this, eventually.

"Your friend," he said. "What is his name?"

She thought about this with the seriousness she brought to all questions. "I call him Rouge-gorge," she said.

Robin. The French word for the small, red-breasted bird, the one that appeared in winter gardens and on Christmas cards, the one that children were taught to love because it was small and bright and came close to human habitation without fear.

"Why Rouge-gorge?" he asked.

"Because of his color," she said. "And because he's small. And because he's not afraid of me." She said this last part with a slight emphasis, as if it were the most important criterion, and he supposed, for a child who had been described as watchful and serious and difficult to befriend, it probably was.

"Where do you see him?" Antoine asked. "On the ship?"

"All over," she said. "But mostly at the front of the ship in the evenings. And below, where it's dark. He likes the dark." She picked up a piece of hardtack and examined it without enthusiasm. "He's very old," she added. "He told me. Very old. Older than the ship."

"Did he?" Antoine said.

"He said he's been waiting for this ship for a long time." She said it simply, a child reporting information, no understanding of it in her face but no fear either. "He said it's important. This crossing. He said things will happen that people will remember."

Antoine's hands were flat on the table in front of him. He was aware of them much like you notice your hands when you are trying to keep them still.

"Marguerite," he said. "Did he say what things?"

She looked at him then with that steady gaze, and there was something in it, not malice, not mischief, but a kind of sorrow that had no business being in the face of an eight-year-old girl.

"He said a storm is coming," she said. "A bad one. He said Some of you will die." She put down the hardtack. "He said I shouldn't be frightened because he'll keep me safe. And you." She paused. "He said you're the most important one. He's been waiting on you the longest to take him to his brothers."

The ship moved through a long, slow swell. Antoine felt it in his legs, the familiar rise and fall.

"Did he say why?" Antoine asked, and his voice was very quiet.

But Marguerite had looked away, her attention caught by her mother returning with the bowls, and she didn't answer, and Antoine did not ask again because he was not sure he wanted the answer in a room full of people.

He became aware, gradually, of a sound he had not noticed over the next thirty seconds. It was faint. A kind of low whisper against the hull, against the deck planking overhead, against the canvas above that. He thought at first it was the rigging. He thought at first it was the wind changing.

Then a drop of water hit the back of his hand.

He looked up. A bead of moisture found its way through a gap in the deck above, and ran along a beam and gathered itself and fell, how water finds every imperfection and exploits it. A single drop, dark against the back of his hand.

Then another. On the table. On the bench beside him.

And then the sound resolved into what it had been all along, what it always was at sea when you finally let yourself hear it properly—the sound of rain. Light rain, the advance guard of the kind of rain that preceded heavier things. The kind of rain that came before storms.

Around him men were looking up, were saying things to each other in low voices, were doing the calculations that sailors do when they feel harsh weather coming.

Antoine looked at Marguerite.

She was eating her hardtack. She did not look up. But the corner of her mouth moved slightly, like mouths do when a person knows something has arrived that they were told was coming, and had found the prediction confirmed, and feel the small, complicated satisfaction of that confirmation even when the thing confirmed was not a good thing.

Antoine got up from the bench. His legs carried him up the ladder and out onto the deck and he stood in the thin gray rain with his face turned up to a sky that had gone the color of a bruise, purple-green and swollen, pressing down on the water from horizon to horizon.

The wind had changed.

He could feel it in the way the ship moved, the swell coming differently now, from the wrong quarter, the kind of shift that meant the weather ahead was not the weather behind. The sailors on deck were moving with purpose, the efficient pre-storm choreography of men who knew what they were looking at and were beginning to prepare for it.

Antoine put his hand in his coat pocket. The ribbon was there, that small red scrap of silk. He held it without taking it out.

He's been waiting for you the longest. To take him to his brothers.

The rain was picking up now. He could hear it on the water around the ship, that particular percussion, and he could see the line of heavier weather on the western horizon, a darkness within the darkness, moving toward them with the slow inexorable patience of something knew perfectly well where you were going to be and intended to be there when you arrived.

He went below to check the lashings on the cargo.

He did not look at the grandmother's box when he passed it.

But he thought about it all the way down the ladder, and he was still thinking about it when the storm arrived three hours later and the hatch slammed shut and the world became noise and darkness and the sound of men praying in two languages to a God who was under no particular obligation to listen.

Chapter Five

The Storm

Antoine de la Mothe Cadillac descended the narrow ladder into the hold, the stench of unwashed bodies and salted provisions hit him like a fist. Three weeks into the Atlantic crossing, and already the ship felt like a powder keg waiting for a spark. The creaking timbers overhead groaned with each swell, a sound that had become as familiar as breathing, though no less unsettling. Below deck, in the dim light filtering through the hatch, twenty-seven men packed themselves into a space meant for twenty.

He steadied himself against a beam as the vessel pitched to starboard. The King's commission, in his trunk upstairs, elegant calligraphy on vellum, sealed with royal wax, promised him governorship of a wilderness fort at the junction of two great lakes. New France. A territory so vast that mapmakers left it mostly blank, filling the empty spaces with speculation and fantasy. But first he needed to survive the crossing with a crew that was already fracturing along fault lines of nationality, superstition, and pride.

"Monsieur Cadillac." Jean-Baptiste Charbonneau emerged from between two hammocks, his face gaunt in the half-light. The carpenter had lost weight on the voyage, as they all had. The provisions Cadillac promised in La Rochelle proved optimistic at best, fraudulent at worst. "You need to speak with the men. There's trouble brewing over the water rations."

The Commandant nodded, though his jaw tightened. This was the third dispute in as many days. "Show me."

They navigated the cramped passages between swaying hammocks and stacked crates, stepping over men who sat playing cards with a worn deck, their movements automatic, mechanical. The ship's rhythmic groaning seemed louder here, deeper in the hold, as though the vessel itself was complaining about its burden. The air was thick and moist, tasting of brine and mildew. Somewhere near the stern, two voices rose in argument, one French, one Flemish. Always the same divisions.

Cadillac found them near the water barrels: Michel Dubois, a Norman sailor with forearms like rope and a temper to match, and Pieter Van der Meer, a Flemish gunner whose family had served the Spanish before shifting allegiance to France. Between them, a wooden cup lay overturned on the deck, its contents spreading in a dark stain.

"He takes double rations," Dubois said, his finger jabbing toward Van der Meer's chest. "I've watched him. Every morning, the Flemish dog fills his cup twice."

"Liar." Van der Meer's accent thickened with anger. "I take what I am given, no more."

"Gentlemen," Cadillac let his voice carry the weight of authority without raising it. Both men turned, and he saw the calculation in their eyes, the measuring of whether this well-dressed nobleman from the upper deck possessed any real power, where in the ship's belly, rank often meant less than fists. "The rations are measured by the quartermaster. If there's theft, we will discover it and punish it. But accusations without proof poison us faster than any thirst."

Dubois spat on the deck. "Fine words, monsieur. But fine words don't fill a man's belly, and they don't wet his throat. We're three weeks out with three more ahead, and already the biscuits are crawling with weevils. The water tastes like iron and piss."

"Then we conserve what we have and pray for rain," Cadillac said. He stepped between the two men, close enough that they could see he wasn't afraid to stand in the narrow space, to put himself within reach of their anger. "Or we can fight each other for scraps and arrive in New France with half our number dead or wounded. I'm sure the Iroquois will appreciate our weakened state."

That landed. He saw it in how Van der Meer's shoulders dropped slightly, and the way Dubois's eyes shifted toward the deck. The Iroquois, the ghost story that haunted every man aboard. The tales from returned voyageurs spoke of torture practices that made European warfare seem civilized: slow fires, flaying, ritual cannibalism. Whether true or exaggerated, the stories served Cadillac's purpose now.

"We share what we have," he continued. "We arrive whole. That is how we survive."

Dubois muttered something under his breath, but nodded. Van der Meer retrieved the cup and moved away. Crisis averted. Temporarily.

Cadillac turned to Charbonneau. "Tell the captain that I suggest we double the watch on the provisions. I want two men with eyes on the stores at all times, one French, one Flemish. They will keep each other honest."

"That will strain our...,"

"Do it."

The carpenter nodded and disappeared into the gloom. Cadillac remained a moment longer, watching the men settle back into their miserable routines. Some slept in their hammocks despite the early hour, preserving energy. Others huddled in small groups, speaking in low voices that stopped when he passed. The divisions were deeper than he'd thought. Language, yes, but also religion: Catholics and Huguenots forced into proximity by the King's will. Old world grudges stuffed into a floating wooden box.

He made his way toward the ladder, exchanging brief words with a few of the men, asking after their health, complimenting a well-maintained musket, reminding them of the land grants waiting for them in the New World. Small gestures. Deliberate. He needed these men functional when they reached Quebec. Needed them unified enough to face whatever waited in that wilderness.

He was halfway up the ladder when the ship lurched violently to port.

Cadillac grabbed the ladder rails as the entire vessel canted at an angle that defied reason. Below, men shouted in alarm. A crate tore loose from its lashing and slid across the deck, slamming into a support beam with a crack like a gunshot. The hammocks swung wildly, men tumbling from them, and the ship heaved again, rising and falling with such violence that Cadillac's stomach lurched.

"Storm!" someone screamed from above. "All hands! Storm!"

The hatch slammed shut.

The hold plunged into near-total darkness. Only the faint glow from two oil lanterns remained, and these swung on their hooks like demented pendulums, casting careening shadows across the suddenly tilting world. The ship groaned, a sound different from before, deeper, agonized. Timber shrieked against timber. Water sprayed through gaps in the planking above, cold and shocking.

Cadillac fought his way back down the ladder as the vessel pitched again. His boots hit the deck just as another massive wave struck the hull. The impact resonated through every board, every beam. The ship rolled, and this time it kept rolling, far enough that Cadillac had to grab a rope to keep from sliding into the port bulkhead where men and cargo piled together in a shouting, cursing heap.

One of the lanterns tore free. It arced through the air in slow motion, trailing flame, before shattering against a stack of barrels. Fire licked up the wood for one heart-stopping moment before the next wave broke over the deck above, and seawater poured through the planking like a waterfall, dousing the flames but soaking everything.

"Get the lanterns secured!" He heard a seaman shout, but his voice was lost in the chaos. The wind above howled like something alive, something hungry. The ship climbed the face of a wave, he could feel it in his legs, the steep upward angle, and then dropped into the trough beyond. His feet left the deck for a sickening instant. When he landed, he heard bone crack somewhere to his left.

A man screamed. Not a shout, not a curse, a genuine scream of agony.

"Light!" Cadillac roars. "I need light!"

Charbonneau appeared with a lantern held high. In its guttering glow, Cadillac saw the source of the screaming: one of the younger sailors, barely eighteen, pinned beneath a water barrel that had torn free from its lashing. The boy's leg bent at an obscene angle. His face had gone white as chalk, lips pulled back from his teeth.

"Get that barrel off him!" Cadillac pushed through the press of bodies, grabbing men by their shoulders, organizing them by pure force of will. "You three, lift on my count! Van der Meer, brace him! Dubois, get rope to secure these damned barrels before they crush us all!"

The ship heaved again, and they had to wait, clinging to whatever they could reach, as the world became a tumbling nightmare of water and darkness and sound. When the vessel finally leveled, relatively speaking, Cadillac counted: "One, two, three, lift!"

The barrel rose. The boy screamed again, a sound that cut through even the storm's fury. They dragged him clear, and Cadillac saw the compound fracture, bone white against red, and knew that leg was lost even if they managed to keep the boy alive.

"Get him to the stern! Make a space!" He turned to find more chaos unfolding: another crate had broken open, scattering their precious flour across the deck where it mixed with seawater into paste. Men were fighting to secure cargo, to keep it from becoming projectiles in the confined space. The ship pitched and rolled with such violence that up and down became suggestions rather than facts.

Cadillac worked among them, lending his strength where needed, his voice cutting through the panic when he could make himself heard. But even as he organized, even as he imposed order on the chaos, he felt it, the helplessness. They were trapped in a wooden box at the mercy of forces beyond any human control. The King's commission meant nothing here. His authority was a fiction that the Atlantic Ocean could erase with a single wave.

Another impact, something striking the hull from outside. Not a wave this time. Something solid. The sound echoed through the hold like a drum, and men froze, their eyes wide in the swinging lantern light.

"Wreckage," Charbonneau said, but his voice carried doubt. "Floating timber, maybe."

Maybe. Or maybe the hull was breached. Maybe they were taking on water faster than the pumps could manage. Maybe this crossing would end here, now, with all of them drowning in the dark while the Atlantic swallowed their ambitions and their bones.

The ship climbed another wave, and Cadillac braced himself against a beam, his hands gripping the rough wood until splinters drove into his palms. Around him, men prayed in French and Flemish, their voices joining in a desperate chorus that transcended their divisions. Catholics and Huguenots alike called out to God, to Mary, to any saint who might hear them through the storm's fury.

When the wave crested and they plunged down the far side, Cadillac caught a glimpse of Dubois, the man who'd been ready to fight over water rations an hour ago, now holding Van der Meer steady as the Flemish gunner tied down a loose cannon that had nearly rolled over two men. Working together because the alternative was death.

But the unity born of terror wouldn't last. Cadillac knew with cold certainty. If they survived this, the divisions would return. The shortages would remain. And he would still be trying to hold together twenty-seven fractious men with nothing but words and the promise of land in a wilderness most of them feared more than they feared drowning.

The injured boy's screaming had subsided to whimpering. Cadillac made his way to the stern through the lurching darkness and knelt beside him. The boy's eyes were glassy with shock. His leg had already started to swell, the flesh around the break turning purple.

"What's your name?" Cadillac asked, though he had to lean close to be heard over the storm.

"Pierre," the boy whispered. Pierre Fontaine, but my friend's call me Parker."

"You'll survive this, Parker." A lie, probably, but a useful one. "When we reach New France, you'll have a story to tell."

The boy nodded, wanting to believe it, and Cadillac felt the weight of that false hope like a stone in his chest. Another responsibility. Another promise he might not be able to keep.

The ship pitched again, and this time Cadillac heard something new beneath the storm's roar: the grinding crack of wood under impossible strain. The mainmast, maybe. Or a yardarm. Something above them was failing, and there was nothing any of them could do but wait in the dark and pray the vessel held together long enough to see morning.

If morning came.

Cadillac closed his eyes for just a moment, allowing himself that single instant of despair, and then opened them again and returned to work. There were lashings to secure, men to organize, injuries to tend. The storm would break, or it wouldn't. They would survive or they would drown. But until the Atlantic made its final judgment, he would assist the crew in maintaining order. He was the commandant, and he would hold these men together.

Even if it killed him.

***

Dr. Thomas Mercer's hands shook as he tore another strip from his already-ruined shirt, the linen parting with a wet sound that made his stomach clench. The fabric was slick with the young sailor's blood, Pierre, the boy's name was Pierre, and the makeshift bandages he'd already applied were soaking through faster than seemed possible. The ship rolled hard to starboard, and Thomas braced his knee against the bulkhead, fighting to keep his position beside the boy sprawled across the common area deck. Around them, the storm's voice was a living thing, shrieking through the timbers with a fury that seemed personal, seemed targeted.

Pierre whimpered, and Dr. Thomas forced his attention back to the compound fracture, the white shard of bone jutting through torn flesh just above the ankle. His medical training, three years as a field surgeon's assistant before the drink had cost him that position, came back in fragments, muscle memory guiding his fingers as he wound the cloth tight enough to staunch the bleeding but not so tight it would kill the foot. The lanterns hanging from the beam overhead swung in wild arcs, throwing their shadows across the walls like dancing demons.

"Easy, lad," Thomas heard himself say, his voice steadier than he felt. "Easy now."

But it wasn't easy. Nothing about this was easy.

The storm had come from nowhere, he'd been topside not twenty minutes before it hit, had seen clear stars in a cloudless sky. Then the wind had risen like something exhaled from the deep, and the rain had come down in sheets that felt solid as fists. Captain Moreau had ordered everyone below, his face gray in the sudden darkness, and they'd barely made it down the ladder before the first wave had struck broadside, sending cargo sliding and men stumbling. The crash of splintering wood. Parker's scream. The smell of fear, sweat and vomiting as the ship pitched and yawed in ways no vessel should move and remain whole.

Thomas tied off the bandage and sat back on his heels, wiping his palms on his trousers. The blood smeared but didn't come off. In the swaying lantern-light, his hands looked painted, theatrical. He flexed his fingers, watching the way the skin pulled tight across his knuckles, noting how the blood had settled into the creases of his palms like some kind of dark map.

Parker had passed out, which was a mercy. Around them, the two dozen other souls trapped below deck had arranged themselves in small clusters, families huddled together, crew members bracing cargo that had come loose, the ship's cook clutching his cooking pot like it was the only solid thing left in the world. Their faces were pale ovals in the darkness, eyes too wide, mouths too tight. Thomas recognized that look. He'd seen it before in field hospitals during the war. The look of people realizing they might die, and soon, and badly.

He pushed himself to his feet, steadying himself against the bulkhead as the ship crested another massive wave. The wood beneath his palm was slick with condensation, cold as a corpse. Through the deck boards above, he could hear the muffled shouts of the skeleton crew still topside, their words lost in the storm's roar but the panic in them clear enough.

Something had broken the crew's unity down here. He could feel it, could see it in the way Moreau's first mate, Renard, a thick-necked Irishman who'd been steady as stone for the entire voyage, kept glancing toward the ladder with something too close to wildness in his eyes. Could see it in the way the passengers had stopped looking to the crew for reassurance and started looking to each other instead, or to nothing at all. A crack had opened, invisible but real, and through it Thomas could sense something seeping in. Not water. Something else.

Fear, yes. But more than fear.

The doctor moved across the common area, his surgeon's instinct driving him to check the other injuries. A woman with a badly bruised shoulder where she'd been thrown against a support beam. A child with a split lip, crying quietly into his mother's skirt. A crewman with a gash across his forehead that looked worse than it was, head wounds always bled like slaughter. Thomas cleaned what he could with strips torn from the bottom of his coat, his hands moving through the familiar motions while his mind turned over the problem that had no suitable answer.

They were trapped down here. The storm gave them no choice about that. But trapped down here with Parker bleeding and moaning, with supplies scattered and the ship groaning like it was trying to tear itself apart, with fear spreading like fever through the cramped space, that was a powder keg. Already he noticed how people were starting to fracture along fault lines. The passengers blamed the crew for not seeing the storm coming. The crew blamed the passengers for being dead weight. The families with children were eying the single water barrel with an arithmetic Thomas recognized: How long will it last? How many of us are there? What happens when it runs out?

He could try to keep them together. Use his medical authority, limited as it was, to give them something to focus on besides their fear. Organize them into shifts: some to tend the injured, some to secure cargo, and some to monitor the water and supplies. Give them tasks, give them purpose, keep their hands busy and their minds occupied. It might work. Probably would work, for a while at least. He'd seen it work in field hospitals when things got desperate.

But it would cost him. He'd have to step forward, take charge, make himself responsible not just for Parker's leg but for all of them. And if things went bad, when things went bad, because in his experience they always did, they'd turn on him. The leader was always the first one thrown overboard when the crowd needed someone to blame. He'd learned that lesson the hard way, learned it when the drink had made his hands shake during a surgery and the patient had died, and suddenly every mistake in the entire field hospital had been laid at his feet.

He moved to the water barrel and dipped his hands in, watching the blood swirl away in dark ribbons. The water was still clean, still cold. He cupped a palmful and drank, tasting salt and iron despite the freshness. His reflection wavered on the water's surface, haggard, hollow-eyed, older than his forty-three years.

Or he could stay small. Keep his head down, tend the injured when asked, but not volunteer for anything more. Let Moreau or Renard handle the leadership, let someone else make the decisions and take the blame. He could fade into the background, just another passenger waiting out the storm, and when the reckoning came, and it would come, he could feel it in his bones, he'd be overlooked. Invisible. Safe.

The thought made him feel dirty in a way the blood hadn't.

But it was practical. Smart, even. He'd stepped forward before, had tried to be the hero, and it had cost him everything: his position, his reputation, his self-respect. What made him think this time would be different? What made him think he had anything left to give these people?

The ship pitched again, harder than before, and someone screamed. Thomas turned to see cargo shifting, a heavy trunk sliding across the deck toward a cluster of children. His body moved before his mind caught up, three strides and he was there, throwing his shoulder against the trunk, boots scrabbling for purchase on the wet planking. The impact drove the air from his lungs, but the trunk stopped, pinned between his weight and the bulkhead.

"Get them back!" he shouted at the nearest crewman. "Secure this properly!"

The crewman stared at him for a heartbeat, then moved, calling for rope. Others joined him. The children were pulled to safety. Thomas stayed where he was, shoulder burning, the trunk's weight solid against his chest, and felt something shift inside him.

Not resolve. Not yet.

But recognition. The recognition that he'd already made his choice made it the moment he'd torn his shirt to bandage Parker's leg. Made it because he couldn't not make it, because whatever he'd lost to the drink and the failures that came after, he apparently hadn't lost the part of him that moved toward the screaming instead of away from it.

Goddamn it.

He waited until the trunk was properly secured, then pushed away from it and walked back to the center of the common area. His voice, when he found it, carried through the storm-sound with an authority he'd thought he'd lost years ago.

"Listen to me," he said. "All of you. We're going to organize. I need volunteers for injury assessment, cargo security, and water rationing. We're going to do this properly, and we're going to do it now, and we're going to keep ourselves together until this damned storm passes."

Faces turned toward him. Brennan's eyes narrowed, calculating. A woman near the back, one of the passengers, well-dressed despite the circumstances, gave a single, sharp nod.

Thomas felt his hands steady. Felt the shaking stop.

"You," he pointed to Brennan. "Get me a count of all injuries, major and minor. You," to the woman who'd nodded, "organize family groups and assign spots where they won't be in the way of shifting cargo. You," to a young crewman whose name he didn't know, "inventory our supplies: food, water, medical kit if there is one. I want numbers, and I want them in five minutes."

They moved. Not quickly, not eagerly, but they moved.

Thomas knelt beside Parker again, checking the bandage, checking the boy's pulse. Still alive. Still breathing. The bone would need proper setting when the storm passed, would need more than Thomas's field-surgery skills could provide, but for now it was enough.

For now, keeping them together was enough.

He'd pay for this decision eventually. Probably sooner rather than later. But as he looked around the cramped, fear-soaked common area, at the faces that had stopped fracturing and started focusing, he found he could live with that cost.

He'd lived with worse.

And through all the chaos, too minor to observe amid injury, screams and moving cargo, all failed to notice Marguerite sitting quietly talking to what appeared to be smoking red coals floating in the air.

Chapter Six

The Morning After

He had slept well, which surprised him.

Not deeply, not without interruption — the storm had seen to that, three hours of violence that had left the ship groaning and the crew shaken and young Parker Fontaine with a leg that would never be quite right again, but well enough that when he came awake just before dawn he felt something approximating rest, which was more than he had expected and more than he probably deserved. He lay on his cot for a moment in the dark, listening to the ship, cataloging the sounds. A habit he always did in the first moments of wakefulness: the changed quality of the swells, lighter now, the storm having blown itself out somewhere in the small hours; the creak of the masts resettling; the low voices of the watch above, tired but steady. The particular silence of a ship that has survived something and knew it.

The grandmother's box was on the shelf where he had put it. He did not look at it when he dressed.

He came up through the hatch into a morning that was doing its best to look innocent.

The sky had gone the pale, washed blue that follows Atlantic storms, the kind of blue that had no depth to it, a sky that had been scoured clean and was still catching its breath. The deck was dark with moisture, puddles standing in the low places where the planking had warped, and the rigging dripped in a slow, irregular percussion that was almost musical if you were in the right frame of mind for it. Antoine stood at the top of the ladder for a moment and breathed it in salt and tar and the faint sweetness of wet rope drying, and felt, briefly and without entirely understanding why, something that was almost like gratitude. They had come through the night. The ship was whole. The men were alive, most unharmed save for the broken bones that would heal or wouldn't, and the Atlantic this morning looked like a thing that had never meant anyone any harm.

He knew better. But the morning made a convincing argument.

Moreau was already on deck, which was not surprising. Antoine suspected the captain slept the way all good captains slept: lightly and with one ear on the ship at all times, so that anything requiring his attention would find him already halfway to vertical before it had finished requiring it. He was moving along the starboard rail with his first mate Renard, the two of them examined a section of the rail that had taken damage in the night, speaking in the low efficient shorthand of men who had worked together long enough to have their own language. He glanced up when Antoine emerged, gave him a nod that acknowledged his existence and communicated nothing else, and returned to his assessment.

This was, Antoine had come to understand, the highest form of approval available from Moreau. He accepted it in the spirit in which it was offered.

He made his way forward, surveying the aftermath with the eye of a man who had learned to read the health of an enterprise in its physical details. The storm had made a mess of the deck — a length of spare canvas that had come loose from its lashing was piled against the forecastle like a drunk sleeping it off, two of the water barrels had shifted and been re-lashed with what looked like hasty knots that would need proper attention, and a section of the port side rigging had developed a tangle that three sailors were currently arguing about in the companionable way of men who disagreed about the best solution but agreed on the urgency. The mainmast was sound. The hull, as far as he could tell from above, was sound. The pumps had kept up with whatever water they'd taken on during the worst of it.

The expedition was intact. Battered, tired, short one able-bodied sailor for the foreseeable future, but intact.

Antoine strolled the deck, hands clasped behind his back, the posture, which he had learned early in his career, communicated authority without aggression, a man surveying what was his, not a man looking for someone to blame. He paused to speak to the men working the rigging tangle, not to advise them but to acknowledge them, which was a different and more important thing. He crouched briefly beside the re-lashed water barrels and checked the knots with his fingers and said nothing about what he found there, only made a mental note to have Charbonneau see to them properly before the sun got high. Small things. The business of the morning after.

It was at the mainmast that he found Bertrand.

The man was working alone, coiling a length of rope that had come free in the night, and he was doing it with the automatic precision of someone whose hands know their job well enough to continue without supervision from the brain, which meant his brain was somewhere else entirely. He did not hear Antoine approach, or if he heard him, chose not to acknowledge it, and Antoine stood and watched him for a moment. The set of his shoulders, the way his eyes were focused on nothing, the particular quality of a man carrying something heavy in a place that didn't show.

"Bertrand," he said.

The sailor looked up. His face went through a quick sequence of adjustments, similar to what faces do when they have been caught off guard. The professional expression slid into place over whatever had been there before. He was a man of perhaps fifty, face the color and texture of old saddle leather, with eyes that had spent decades looking at horizons and had arrived at a settled relationship with distance.

"Commandant," he said. Not *Captain* — Antoine had made that correction on the second day, and Bertrand had absorbed it without comment. A careful man. "Morning."

"Hell of a night," Antoine said.

"Aye." Bertrand went back to the rope, the coils building with rhythmic efficiency. "Ship held."

"She did." Antoine leaned against the mast, a posture that said *I'm not going anywhere* without making it a confrontation. "How's the crew?"

A pause in the coiling. Brief, but there. "Tired," Bertrand said. "Shaken some. Parker's leg got them..." he considered his words "...thoughtful."

Thoughtful was doing a great deal of work in that sentence. Antoine let it stand.

"Thomas Mercer did well last night," Antoine said. "With Parker."

"He did." Bertrand's hands slowed slightly. "Good man to have aboard, turns out. Wouldn't have guessed it, looking at him." Another pause, longer this time, the rope was still going in his hands. "There's talk," he said, not looking up. "Below. It started last night during the worst of it. Probably nothing."

"What kind of talk?"

Bertrand's jaw worked for a moment. He was a man who chose words carefully and resented being made to produce them before they were ready, and Antoine waited, because he had learned that patience was a better tool than pressure with this particular type of man.

"The dreams," Bertrand said finally. "Some of the men have been having... " he stopped, started again. "Bad dreams. Same sort of thing. A figure, they say. Small. Red eyes." He said it in the manner a man said something he knows sounds foolish but is reporting faithfully anyway, his voice carrying the slight defensiveness of a reliable witness who expects not to be believed. "Jacques had it three nights running before the storm. Woke screaming the second time, woke half the berth with him. And it's not just Jacques."

Antoine said nothing. He was aware of his own face and what it was displaying, and was making sure it was doing the right thing, which was mild interest, the expression of a man receiving information that he will assess rationally and respond to reasonably.

"I don't dream much myself," Bertrand continued, the words coming a little easier now that he'd started. "Never have. But last night, in the storm..." he stopped again, and something moved briefly across his face that Antoine had not seen there before. "I heard something. Below the noise of the storm, below the wind. Something that wasn't the ship." He looked up then, and his eyes were steady and direct and more troubled than the rest of his face was letting on. "It was laughing."

The morning was bright and the deck was full of men working and the ship was moving through gentle swells under a washed-out blue sky, and Antoine was a man of the new century, a rational man, a man with a royal commission and a mission of considerable importance and no time for the superstitions of sailors who had been frightened by a storm.

He said: "Men hear things in bad weather. The mind plays tricks when it's frightened and exhausted."

Bertrand nodded slowly. "Aye," he said. "That's what I told Jacques."

A beat of silence between them.

"Is he all right?" Antoine asked. "Jacques."

"He's working," Bertrand said, which among this particular class of men was the answer that meant *he is not all right, but he is functional, and that is the best available outcome.*

"Keep an eye on him," Antoine said. "On all of them. And if the talk gets...," he searched for the right word "...louder, you come to me. Before it goes anywhere else."

Bertrand looked at him for a moment. There was something in the look, some questions being considered and then set aside, and Antoine had the feeling, familiar and unwelcome, of being assessed by someone who knew more than they were saying, or suspected more than they could prove.

"Aye, Commandant," Bertrand said, and went back to his rope.

Antoine pushed off the mast and continued his circuit of the deck. He moved unhurriedly, stopping here and there, speaking to men, asking about the damage, keeping his voice in the register that communicated everything was in hand and the morning was ordinary and the night had been nothing that capable men could not put behind them by noon.

He was very good at this. He had spent twenty years becoming very good at this.

He reached the stern and stood at the rail and looked at the water, which was green gray in the morning light and going about its business with the total indifference of something that had been doing what it did long before the first ship was built and intended to continue long after the last one sank. He gripped the rail and breathed in and out, the salt air filling his lungs and leaving them.

It was laughing.

Somewhere below him, in the dark of his berth, the grandmother's box sat on its shelf. He had put it there several days ago, moved it from the trunk after the second business with the cord, told himself he wanted to know where it was. He had not opened it. He was not ready to open it.

He wondered, standing at the stern rail in the clean-washed morning, how much longer he could afford not to be ready.

A burst of laughter from the men working the port side rigging: something genuinely funny had happened with the tangle, or been said about it, and for a moment the deck was briefly, unexpectedly light. Antoine turned and looked at them, at the easy way they leaned into each other's space, at the release of it, the simple animal pleasure of men who had been frightened together in the dark and had made it to morning.

It wouldn't last. He knew that. The fractures were already there. He could see them, how you could see the lines in old timber before it gave way, and a dreadful night and a broken leg and whatever Bertrand wasn't quite saying about the dreams had not improved the structural situation. The ship was sound. The men were another question.

But for now, the laughter was real, and the morning was bright, and they were moving westward at a reasonable pace toward a place that existed so far only in royal dispatches and his own ambition, and that was enough to work with.

Antoine de la Mothe Cadillac, commandant of the expedition to establish Fort Pontchartrain du Détroit, straightened his coat and turned away from the rail and went to find Charbonneau about those water barrel lashings.

The morning had work in it. He intended to use every hour of it.

Chapter Seven

The Hold

The door came open without knocking.

That was the first thing — the absence of the knock, which told Antoine everything about the nature of what was coming before Moreau had said a single word. In Antoine's experience, men who knocked were men who still believed in the possibility of a civil outcome. Men who did not knock had already arrived at a different conclusion.

Moreau filled the doorway with two of his crew behind him, and his face was the face of a man who had decided sometime in the night and had spent the intervening hours becoming more certain of it rather than less. He was still in his coat from the watch, which meant he had not slept, and his eyes had the particular flat quality of exhaustion pushed past the point where it affected judgment and into the territory where it simply became a permanent condition, like the color of the sea.

"Goddamn you, Cadillac," he said. Not loud. Moreau was never loud. Which made it worse. "Didn't I tell you? Didn't I tell you specifically, with words, that if you could not secure that trunk, I would place it in the hold myself?"

Antoine had been awake. He had been awake for some time, lying in the dark listening to the sounds of the ship, to the particular sound that had been happening somewhere below him at irregular intervals since the second watch bell, the hollow wooden percussion that he recognized yet still tried not to think about. He had been working on what he intended to say when this moment arrived.

None of it seemed adequate now.

"Captain..." he started.

"I gave you two nights," Moreau said. "Two nights and a direct order and my personal intervention and the benefit of every doubt a man in my position is capable of extending. And last night..." he stopped, and something moved in his face that was not quite anger and not quite something else, a composite of exhaustion and frustration and, underneath both of those, a thread of something Antoine did not yet have a name for "...last night my watch reported that three men refused to go below because of the sound. Three men. On a working vessel. In the North Atlantic."

He stepped back and gestured to the two sailors behind him, a short, economical gesture that meant *now.*

"Wait," Antoine said. He was on his feet; he had not remembered standing. "There are documents in there. Commission papers. Instruments. If they're not properly..."

"Then you should have secured the trunk when I asked you to," Moreau said. "Take it."

The two sailors moved past Antoine with the careful efficiency of men executing an order they had been given clearly and had no interest in complicating with hesitation. They were not rough with it. That was the thing that struck Antoine as they lifted his trunk between them, the almost deliberate care they took, as if they were afraid of it and were covering the fear with professionalism. They did not look at

Antoine. They did not look at each other. They looked at the trunk, carried it, and left.

Moreau looked at Antoine for a moment after they had gone. Just a moment.

"When we reach Quebec," he said, "you may reclaim it under supervision. Until then." He left the rest of the sentence unfinished, which was worse than finishing would have been.

He left. He did not close the door behind him.

Antoine stood in his berth in the gray morning light and looked at the shelf where the grandmother's box was not, because the grandmother's box was now in the trunk, which was now in the hold, and he had not opened it, and he was not ready, and it didn't matter anymore whether he was ready or not because the box was gone and whatever was of import was gone with it, down into the belly of the ship where the ballast groaned and the darkness was the particular absolute darkness of a space that the sun had never touched.

He sat down on his cot.

He sat there for quite a long time.

* * *

That night, the entire ship heard it.

Not the careful intermittent knocking of the previous nights — this was different in character and in scale, a rhythmic concussive banging that came up through the hull timbers and into the planking of the deck and into the feet of every man standing on it, something you felt in your bones before you heard it with your ears. It started an hour after the second watch bell, and it did not stop. It did not vary. It simply continued, regular as a heartbeat, patient as a tide.

Antoine was on deck within minutes. Half the crew was already there, most of the passengers, standing in the dark with the confused and frightened expressions of people who have been woken by something they cannot immediately account for and have discovered that being awake does not make it better. The sound rose through the ship like something alive. Like something insisting. Wanting to get out.

Moreau appeared from the stern passage, took in the assembled faces, and for once in Antoine's experience looked briefly at a loss...just briefly, the duration of a single breath, before his face closed back down into its habitual weathered competence.

He turned to his first mate. "Renard. Four men. The hold." He looked at the assembled crew. "The rest of you, back to your berths or your watches. This ship does not stop because of a loose crate."

The explanation landed badly, and he knew it. Antoine could see him know it, but it was the only explanation available, and Moreau was a man who worked with what was available. The crew dispersed with the reluctant shuffle of people who were obeying because the alternative had not yet fully presented itself.

Renard chose his four men with the deliberate care of a man who was not going to explain his criteria but had them. He took the bosun, a solid Breton named Gauthier, and two of the more senior deckhands, Mercier and a Flemish gunner named Picard who had the broad shoulders and incurious face of a man who had handled difficult situations before and expected to handle them again. They went below with two lanterns between them and the particular determined stride of men performing a task they considered beneath their dignity but would execute perfectly, regardless.

Antoine stood at the hatch and listened.

The banging continued for perhaps two minutes after they went below. Then it stopped.

Silence. The ship moved through its swells. Water against the hull. Rigging in the wind.

Then, from below, voices. Gauthier's voice, carrying the flat tone of professional report: *It's the latch. The mechanism's faulty. We're securing it now.* A pause. The sound of something being done. *Right. That's... yes. That'll hold.*

More silence. Longer this time. The quality of a job completed, men turning to leave, the satisfying closure of a problem solved.

Then the banging came back.

Not the gradual resumption of something that had been imperfectly stopped, but immediately, fully, at exactly the same volume and rhythm as before, as if something had been waiting with its breath held for the precise moment when the men had turned their backs.

From below, Antoine heard Gauthier say something he couldn't make out. Then Mercier's voice, higher: *What in the name of...*

Then nothing for three seconds.

Then screaming.

* * *

It was not one voice. That was the first thing that registered, and it registered in Antoine's body before his mind had processed it, a cold that started at the base of his spine and moved outward. It was multiple voices, all of them at once, the sound that a group of men produced when something had happened that had bypassed that part of the brain that manages composure and gone directly to the part that simply responds. Raw. Uncontrolled. The sound of men who had lost the ability to consider how they sounded.

And underneath it — threaded through it, woven into it with the intimacy of something that belonged there was laughter. High and thin and full of a delight so pure it was obscene. The laughter of something that was enjoying itself enormously.

Antoine was moving before he had decided to move. He heard Moreau behind him, heard the captain's boots on the ladder, and they went down together without speaking because there was nothing to say. The passage to the hold was narrow and dark and the sound was getting louder as they moved toward it, the screaming and the laughter both braided together in a way that made the passage feel like a throat they were descending into.

The hold door was shut.

Antoine hit it with his shoulder without slowing, and it did not move. Not locked. He could feel that, could feel the latch sitting in its cradle, not engaged — just shut, with a resistance that had nothing to do with the mechanism and everything to do with something on the other side that did not want it opened. He hit it again. Moreau's weight joined his. The door absorbed both of them and remained where it was.

Through the small porthole in the door's upper section, the glass thick and salt-hazed, they could see the inside of the hold in fragments, lit and unlit, bright and dark, the rhythm of it wrong until Antoine understood that what he was seeing was the muzzle flash of pistols firing in an enclosed space. Flash. Dark. Flash. Dark. The screaming had changed in character, some of the voices stopping and others continuing, and the ones that continued were not the voices of men who were frightened anymore, but of men who had entered some territory that did not have a name that Antoine knew.

Something hit the porthole from the inside.

Blood.

It ran down the glass in the slow thick way that liquids run down cold glass, and Antoine stood with his hands on the door and watched it and the laughter from inside rose in pitch, delighted, thrilled, much how a child's laughter rises when a game reaches its best moment, and he pulled at the door with both hands now and it still would not move and he could hear Moreau behind him praying in a low continuous undertone in the particular French of a man who has not prayed in a very long time and has discovered he remembers it anyway.

Then the laughter stopped.

The silence that replaced it was not an ordinary silence. It was the silence of a room in which something had been completed, a task finished, an account settled. It had weight and finality and no mercy in it anywhere.

The door then swung open on its own.

Chapter Eight

What The Dark Showed Them

Gauthier went first down the ladder, which was his right as bosun and his habit as a man who had spent thirty years going first into spaces that other men were reluctant to enter. He had been in burning holds and flooded bilges and the kind of tight dark spaces that made other men's throats close up, and he had never once felt anything he would have called fear in those places, only the focused attention of a man with a job to do. He was proud of this. It was one of the few things about himself that he was straightforwardly proud of without qualification.

He would think about that pride later, in the seconds he had left for thinking. He would think about it with something that was almost amusement.

Mercier came down behind him, then Picard with the second lantern, then young Fournier, who was seventeen and had volunteered because he was seventeen and did not yet know which things were worth volunteering for. The hold received them with its usual smell — salt pork and bilge water and the sweetness of old rope — and Gauthier held his lantern up and looked at the trunk.

It was sitting where they'd put it that morning, against the port wall between two stacks of provision crates, exactly where Moreau had told them to put it. Nothing wrong with it. Nothing moving. Just a trunk, large, dark wood with iron fittings, sitting on the deck of a ship the way trunks sit when they are trunks and nothing more.

"Right," Gauthier said. "Let's see what the famous trunk of Monsieur Cadillac thinks it's doing."

Gauthier crouched in front of the trunk and examined the latch. The mechanism was old, the kind of fittings that had been made to last rather than made to be elegant, heavy iron with a pivot that he could see had some wear in it. He pressed the latch down and felt it seat. He pressed it again. It was firm.

"Latch is loose," he said, for Mercier's benefit. "Pivot's worn. Every time the ship takes a roll, it's probably—" he pressed it a third time "—working free. Simple enough."

"Can we fix it?" Mercier asked.

"Don't need to fix it. Just need to make sure it's properly seated." He pressed it down and held his thumb on it and looked around. "Fournier. There's a coil of rope on the forward stack. Bring me an arm's length."

Fournier went. He was back in thirty seconds with the rope, and Gauthier threaded it through the latch and tied it off in the same manner he tied everything, which was correctly and permanently. He tested it with both hands, putting real weight into it. The latch did not move.

"Right," he said, standing. "That'll hold."

He turned to leave. Mercier turned. Picard turned. Fournier was already facing the ladder.

The banging came back.

Mercier felt it before he heard it — in his feet, in the planking, that percussive thud transmitted through the wood. He turned around. The rope was on the floor. The latch was open. The trunk lid was rising and falling, rising and falling, with the slow, deliberate rhythm of something breathing. Or something showing that it could breathe if it wanted to. Rising and falling on its own, with no hand on it, with no mechanism that any of them could see, just the lid moving up and coming back down and moving up again, patient and rhythmic, like a mouth opening and closing, like a thing that was trying to say something and had all the time in the world to say it.

Gauthier stood still.

In thirty years, he had not felt it. This was what he was thinking. In thirty years of dark holds and burning ships and water coming in through places water should not be coming in, he had not felt it.

He was feeling it now.

"Close it," Picard said. His voice was level. He was a gunner, and gunners were trained to be level.

Gauthier stepped forward and put both hands on the trunk lid and pushed it down.

It went down. He felt the resistance of it, not the resistance of a mechanism but the resistance of something that was considering the question, weighing his effort against its own inclination, and then deciding — not because it was forced, because it was not forced, Gauthier was a strong man but the strength in that lid was not mechanical — to allow it.

The latch seated.

He did not lift his hands from the lid.

The trunk was still.

Around him, he could hear Mercier breathing. He could hear Fournier, who was seventeen, trying not to make any sound at all and not entirely succeeding. He could hear Picard behind him, steady and controlled, and the sound of Picard's pistol being drawn from its holster, because Picard was a man who had learned to respond to the unknown with the vocabulary he had been given, and the vocabulary he had been given was powder and lead.

"All right," Gauthier said. Quietly. "We're going to the ladder. We're going up. Nobody runs."

He lifted his hands from the lid.

The lid opened.

Not fast. Not violently. Slowly, with the same awful deliberateness, any sleeping thing opens its eyes. It rose to forty-five degrees and stopped there, and from inside came a sound that was not the sound of documents settling or instruments shifting against each other. It was a low sound. Low, rhythmic and warm, similar to how something is warm when it has been in an enclosed space for a long time and has filled that space with itself.

It was, Gauthier realized with a clarity that he would have preferred not to have breathing.

Something in the trunk was breathing.

"Ladder," he said, and this time his voice did not sound the way he had spent thirty years making it sound, and he did not apologized for that because there was no time. "Now. Move!"

They moved. Four men toward a ladder that was fifteen feet away across a hold that had been fifteen feet across thirty seconds ago and was somehow not fifteen feet across anymore, the distance wrong in a way that he couldn't locate in any specific measurement, just the sense that the space between them and the ladder was not behaving like space should behave, and that each step was not covering the ground it should be covering.

Mercier reached it first. His foot found the first rung.

And the trunk lid slammed shut.

In the sudden silence after the slam, in the half-second before anything else happened, Gauthier looked at the trunk. He looked at it because he was the kind of man who looked at things, who had built his usefulness on looking at things directly and reporting accurately what he had seen.

The lid was closed. The latch was open. And in the gap, in the thin line of darkness between the lid and the body of the trunk, the darkness that should have been just darkness, that should have been the interior of a wooden box containing documents and instruments and the personal effects of Antoine de la Mothe Cadillac — in that gap: something stared back at him.

Eyes, malevolent and piercing red eyes. Like the red of iron pulled from a forge, the red of something that produced its own light because it had no need for borrowed light, the red of a color that had no business existing in the dark of a ship's hold in the North Atlantic in the year seventeen hundred. Each blinking sliver were points of red, unwavering, and fixed on his face with an attention so complete and so specific that it felt like a hand on his jaw, turning his head, making sure he was looking directly at it.

Making sure he knew it was looking at him.

Then something that mankind might describe as a face grinned.

He knew it grinned because he saw the teeth. White and numerous ivory pincers arranged in a smile that understood the geometry of smiling without understanding what smiling was for, a smile that had learned the shape of the expression without learning the feeling behind it nor cared about the difference.

"Mother of God," Mercier said from the ladder.

* * *

It came out of the trunk much as darkness comes out of a room when you open the door — not rushing, not pouring, simply *expanding* into the available space as if it had been folded and compressed there, waiting for the lid to give it room. It was small. Gauthier registered this with the part of his brain that was still registering things in an organized fashion: small, the size of a child, no taller than his hip, hunched in the way of something that had spent a long time in low spaces and had adapted to them.

It was the color of dried blood and reeked of the same.

It wore a tattered coat. The coat was red, a red so dark it was almost black, and it moved similarly to how shadows move, not not-fabric. Its hands — and Gauthier saw the hands, he would always see the hands, he would see them until he could see nothing anymore — were long-fingered and dark and ended in nails that were black at the tips like how nails go black when the flesh beneath them has died.

It stood in the trunk, and it looked at them, and its expression expressed something that had been patient for a very long time and was experiencing, now, the pleasure of no longer having to be.

Fournier went for the ladder. He was seventeen, and he had good instincts, and he moved faster than any of them.

The thing moved faster.

It did not cross the hold. It was at the trunk, and then it was at the ladder, the transit between the two points happening in the space between one heartbeat and the next. Gauthier watched as Forunier's body rose into the air and tossed back and forth across the hold. Fournier hit something that was not the ladder and was not the wall and was not any surface that in the fleeting darkness Gauthier could identify, and the sound of his body smashing against the ships floor made was not a sound Gauthier had heard a human body make before.

Fournier landed against the port hull, then slid down it and did not get up.

Picard shot it.

The muzzle flash filled the hold with white light for a single terrible instant Gauthier saw everything — the thing in its red coat, unchanged, the ball having passed through it or around it or simply having failed to engage with it in any way that mattered; Mercier frozen on the ladder with both hands on the rungs and his face turned back over his shoulder; Fournier on the floor, not moving; and the thing looking at Picard with an expression that was not anger at being shot, not pain, nor surprise but amusement.

Picard shot it again.

The second flash. The second sound. The thing had not moved, nor had it been moved. It tilted its head similar to how a dog tilts its head when it is hearing something at a frequency that humans cannot hear, and its red eyes moved from Picard to Gauthier, and its grin widened by a precise and measured degree, and it took one step forward.

"The door!" Gauthier shouts. "Mercier — the door, get the..."

Mercier dropped from the ladder and ran for the hold door and hit it with both hands and it did not open, and Gauthier knew from the sound of it, from the flat sound it made under Mercier's palms, that it would not open, that whatever was in this hold with them had made a decision about the door and the decision was final.

Through the porthole in the door's upper section, he could see light. Lantern light from the passage outside. Moving. Getting closer.

He could see faces.

***

Antoine saw Mercier's face in the porthole and hit the door with his shoulder and the door absorbed him completely, took his weight and gave nothing back, and he hit it again because there was nothing else to do and Moreau's weight came in beside him and the door remained where it was.

Through the porthole he could see the hold in fragments. The lanterns inside swinging wildly now, the light chaotic, strobing with the muzzle flashes from Picard's pistol. He could hear the screaming and he could hear the laughter and he could see Mercier's hands on the other side of the porthole glass, the palms flat against it, and Mercier's mouth was open, and he was saying something that Antoine could not hear through the glass and through the screaming and through the laughter that rose through all of it in the manner smoke rises, finding the top of every space.

He saw Mercier pulled back from the porthole.

He did not see what pulled him.

The interior of the porthole glass exploded in red.

***

Gauthier lasted longer than the others. His endurance was not courage, or at least not only courage — it was the stubbornness of a man who has spent thirty years refusing to be beaten by the sea and had applied that same refusal to everything else in his life, a generalized stubbornness that did not distinguish well between rational and irrational persistence. He lasted long enough to see Mercier go. Lasted long enough to see Picard's pistol prove itself useless a third and fourth time until the pistol was empty and Picard threw it at the creature because there was nothing else to throw.

He pressed himself against the hull and he looked at the door and through the porthole he could see the shadows of men outside, trying to get in, and he wanted to tell them not to bother, that the door would not open until it was ready to open, that whatever was in this hold with him operated on a schedule that none outside had been consulted about.

The thing stood in the center of the hold in its red coat draped in the blood of his men and looked at him.

Just at him, now. The others were beyond looking at. It had been thorough.

It was toying with him. He understood the intentionality of the act, that it was letting him have this moment — this moment of clarity, this moment of knowing exactly what was in the hold with him and what was going to happen and that there was nothing between him and it, not distance, not locked doors, not the thirty years of stubbornness that had gotten him this far — a moment it wanted him to have. Because the knowing was, Gauthier suspected, was the part it enjoyed most.

He thought about his daughters, the way fathers think about their wives and children in the final moments of things.

He even thought about that fucking compass sitting wrong in the captain's pocket. Who thinks of such things before they die?

He thought about the little girl at the rail, talking to something he couldn't see, and how she had not looked afraid, not once, not even slightly.

He understood that too now. Understood what she had been talking to and why she had not been afraid and what it meant that she was not afraid. It meant the thing could be gentle when it chose to be. It meant that gentleness was a choice.

It took one step toward him and looked into the red demonic face of the creature, and gentleness did not appear.

He did not close his eyes. He was a man who had spent thirty years looking at things directly.

He looked.

Chapter Nine

The Aftermath

Antoine went in first.

He would never be entirely able to account for what made him go first, whether it was responsibility, obligation, or simply the fact that he was closest to the door when it opened and his legs were already moving. He went in with his lantern held up and what he saw in the yellow circle of its light he saw all at once, completely, in the single moment before his mind began the work of refusing to fully process it.

They had been arranged.

That was what registered before anything else, before the specifics, before the details that he would spend the rest of his life not being able to stop seeing: the deliberateness of it. The four men — what remained of the four men — had been arranged with a care that was somehow worse than the alternative would have been. Worse, because it implied consideration. Worse, because it implied that something had taken its time.

Like wood, he thought. Stacked like wood for burning, the pieces interlocking, fitting together with a precision that spoke of thought and intention and something that understood geometry and the science of assembly.

Behind him, someone was sick. He heard it distantly. His focus shifted like when your attention has narrowed to a single point. He heard Moreau's voice, very quiet, saying something that might have been a command, or might have been a prayer, or might have been both. He heard feet on the ladder above as more of the crew came down, drawn by the silence that had followed the screaming, and he heard the sounds those men made when they saw what he was looking at.

He heard laughter.

Very faint. Very distant. Already receding, like the sound of a bell that has been rung in another room. Not triumphant anymore — something more like satisfied. The sound of something that had what it wanted and was not, for the moment, hungry.

Antoine stood in the hold of La Vigilante and looked at what had been four men and breathed through his nose and did not look away, because looking away would mean something he was not yet prepared for, and after a long time that might have been thirty seconds or ten minutes he turned and went back up the ladder and out through the hatch onto the deck.

The air up top was cold and tasted of salt and the approaching dawn, the sky in the east began its slow negotiation with the dark. The crew had gathered, as was the way people observe spectacle and how people gather after disasters, not quite together, not quite apart, the clustering of bodies that wants the comfort of proximity without the obligation of speech.

Antoine stood at the rail and put his hands on the wood and breathed.

He only became aware of her gradually, similar to how he noticed her that first morning at the dock — peripherally, incompletely, the sense of a presence before the recognition of the specific presence. He turned his head.

Marguerite was on the deck.

She was standing near the mainmast in the gray pre-dawn light, and she was doing what Bertrand had seen her doing at the forecastle rail, and what she had been doing, Antoine now understood, on and off since the first day out from La Rochelle. She was talking. Quietly, her head tilted at an angle, in the same manner children tilt their heads when they are listening to something and responding to what they hear.

As he watched, she stopped. She turned and looked at him. At Moreau, who had come up behind Antoine. At the assembled crew, some of whom had followed Antoine's gaze and were now looking at her with the complicated expressions of people who have just experienced something that had destroyed their relationship with ordinary explanations and were now prepared to find significance in everything.

She looked at Antoine with that expression — the patient, waiting one, the one that said *I knew you would come around to this eventually* — and she then said to Moreau, in the clear carrying voice of a child who has not yet learned to modulate her volume for adult comfort:

"Robin said you should give the trunk back to Monsieur Cadillac."

No one spoke.

Marguerite then turned in a matter-of-fact manner to find her mother and left the men to their musings.

Antoine looked at Moreau.

Moreau looked at Antoine.

Between them, unspoken, the acknowledgment of something that neither man had words for yet, something that had come aboard with them in the harbor at La Rochelle and had been patient, very patient, waiting for the moment when its patience would be recognized for what it was.

Not waiting.

Settling in.

The sun came up over the edge of the world and the light that fell on the deck of La Vigilante was the ordinary light of an Atlantic morning and showed everything clearly, which was the worst thing about it, and somewhere below them in the hold the trunk sat among what was left of four men and waited, the same way it had always waited, with the brass clasp closed and the grandmother's box inside it and the paper in his grandmother's hand with its three underlined words that Antoine had not yet read, that he had been too careful and too proud or too frightened to read, that he was going to have to read now because there was nothing left to hide behind.

He was out of time.

He now realized he had been out of time, since La Rochelle.

Ne laisse jamais le Rouge te nommer deux fois.

Chapter Ten

The Reckoning

They buried what remained of the four men before the sun had fully cleared the horizon, which was not so much a burial as a committal — canvas and rope and the captain's words spoken fast and low, like how prayers are spoken when the man saying them is uncertain they will be received. Father Lescaut stood at the rail with his book open and his eyes moving across the page without, Antoine suspected, seeing any of it. The crew stood in the particular silence of men who had seen something that had rearranged the furniture of their understanding and had not yet worked out how to move through the new configuration.

Then Moreau said: *My cabin. Now.* And looked at Antoine in a way that made the word *now* redundant.

* * *

There were six of them in the captain's quarters, which was four more than the space was designed to accommodate comfortably. Moreau behind his chart table. Renard to his left, first mate's prerogative. Father Lescaut against the starboard wall with his book still in his hands, closed now, held against his chest like a small shield. Charbonneau the carpenter, who had been one of the first men down the ladder after the door opened and whose face had not fully recovered its color since. Bertrand, who had asked to be present and whom Moreau had permitted because Bertrand was the kind of man whose presence in a room made it more honest. And Antoine, standing because there was nowhere left to sit.

The silence lasted approximately four seconds before Charbonneau broke it.

"You knew," he said. Not a question. Not quite an accusation. Something in between: the tone of a man presenting evidence and inviting the defendant to explain it. "You knew something was in that trunk."

"I didn't know—"

"You fought to keep it," Renard said. "When the captain moved it. You fought him."

"I fought to keep my commission documents and my navigational instruments," Antoine said. "Which is a rational response to—"

"Four men are dead." Charbonneau's voice went up on the last word and then came back down, controlled with visible effort. "Gauthier has been on this ship for eleven years. Eleven years. His daughters are in Brest. Someone will have to write to them and I don't—" he stopped. Pressed his mouth closed. Started again. "Someone will have to write to them."

The room absorbed this. Outside, the Atlantic moved against the hull with its usual indifference.

"What was in the trunk, Cadillac?" Moreau said. His voice was very quiet, which meant he was very serious, which meant the conversation had arrived at the part Antoine had been navigating toward since the door of his berth had come open without a knock that morning.

"My grandmother's box," Antoine said. "I don't know exactly what's in it. I haven't opened it."

The silence that followed this was of a different quality than the previous one.

"You haven't—" Renard began.

"I was not ready to open it," Antoine said, and heard how that sounded, and continued before anyone could said what it sounded like. "My grandmother left it to me with instructions that I was not prepared to take seriously until—" he stopped. Looked at the floor. Looked back up. "Until recently."

"What kind of instructions?" Father Lescaut asked. It was the first thing the priest had said. He had a careful voice, a listener's voice, the kind that gathered information before forming conclusions. Antoine found he was grateful for it.

"Protections," Antoine said. "Against the thing she called the Nain Rouge. The red dwarf." He looked at Moreau. "The thing in the hold."

"The Nain Rouge," Lescaut repeated. He drawled it, tasting the words. "I know the stories. The voyageurs' demon. The harbinger."

"It is not a harbinger," Antoine said. "It doesn't appear before disaster. It causes it. There is a difference, and the difference matters."

"What I want to know," Bertrand said, from his position by the door, in the level voice of a man who has decided that being level is the only remaining useful contribution he can make, "is why it's on this ship. Specifically. Why us? Why now?"

Every face in the room turned to Antoine.

He told them. Not everything — not the covenant documents, not the full weight of what his grandmother had understood about the family's history with the creature — but enough. The family name. The generations of it. The box he had carried aboard and had not opened because opening it would have meant accepting something he had spent his adult life refusing to accept. He told them about the compass. About the cord on the floor. About the brass clasp standing open in the morning light.

When he finished, the room was quiet for a long moment.

Then Charbonneau said: "The little girl."

***

They had known, without discussing it, that the conversation would come to Marguerite. She was the variable that none of them had an explanation for, the element that didn't fit any framework they had available — not the priest's framework, not the captain's, not the carpenter's. A child who spoke to it. Who called it by a pet name. Who had told them, in the clear, carrying voice of a child who has not learned to soften things, that Robin said to give the trunk back.

Father Lescaut went to find Céleste.

He had been gone for ten minutes. When he returned, the mother was with him, with Marguerite at her side and the expression of a woman who has agreed to something she is not certain she should have agreed to. She positioned herself beside her daughter with the physical precision of a parent who intends to intervene at the first sign that intervention is warranted.

Marguerite looked around the room at each of them in turn. She did not appear intimidated. She appeared, if anything, faintly satisfied, the way a child appears when adults have finally arrived at the conversation the child has been waiting for.

"Marguerite," Father Lescaut said, crouching to her level with the practiced ease of a man who had spent years in parishes with children, "can you tell us about your friend? The one you call Robin?"

"He doesn't like that name," she said. "I call him that. He lets me because—" she considered "—he says I'm the only one who doesn't make him feel like something to be afraid of." She glanced at Antoine. "The rest of you are afraid of him."

"He's killed four men," Charbonneau said flatly.

Céleste put a hand on his arm. He subsided.

"He says they shouldn't have been in his room," Marguerite said. The simplicity of it was the worst part — not cruelty, just the straightforward relaying of information, the way children relay things they've been told by adults they trust. "He says the trunk is his room. He says it was rude."

"His room," Moreau repeated.

"He's been in it for a long time," the girl said. "Since before Monsieur Cadillac had it." She looked at Antoine again. "He says your grandmother knew. He says she put the things in the box to keep him company. Or to keep him small." She tilted her head. "He wasn't sure which. He said she was clever, and he respected her even though he didn't like her."

Lescaut looked at Antoine. Antoine said nothing.

"What else does he say?" the priest asked Marguerite. "About what he wants. About why he's here."

Marguerite was quiet for a moment, quiet as if trying to remember something accurately and take the responsibility seriously.

"He says Monsieur Cadillac knows why he's here," she said. "He says to ask him." She paused. "He says you can live in the day. But the night belongs to him." She said it without drama, without the weight the words deserved, similar to the delivery of a message you don't fully understand but are being careful to get right. "He said Monsieur Cadillac's grandmother wrote it all down. He said to go and get the letter."

The room turned to Antoine again.

"The box," Antoine said. "The letter is in the box."

"Which is in the hold," Renard said.

"Yes."

The word sat there. Everyone in the room understood what it meant. The hold, where four men had been arranged like timber. The hold, where the trunk sat with its brass clasp and whatever was inside it and whatever the grandmother's cramped handwriting had been trying to tell him for however many years she had been dead.

Moreau looked at Antoine for a long moment. Something moved in his face — not forgiveness, not absolution, nothing as clean as either of those. Something more complicated. The look of a man who has arrived at a situation that exceeds the available frameworks and has decided that the only remaining option is to proceed.

"You'll go tonight," Moreau said. "Before the second watch bell, while there's still light in the passage. You'll go alone."

"Captain—" Renard started.

"Alone," Moreau said. "Because it hasn't taken him yet and I am not sending more men into that hold." He looked at Antoine. "Whatever it wants from you, it wants it from you specifically. Which means you are the only one it has any reason not to kill."

The logic was sound and terrible, and Antoine could not argue with it.

He looked at Marguerite. She was looking back at him with that expression — the waiting one, the one that had been waiting since La Rochelle, since the dock, since the moment she had pressed a red ribbon into his hand and told him it was for luck.

"Robin says you've been ready for a long time," she said. "He says you just didn't know it yet."

Her mother took her by the hand and led her out. The door closed behind them.

The six remaining men stood in the captain's quarters while the ship moved under them and the Atlantic went about its ancient business outside the hull, and no one said anything for a while, because there was nothing to say that improved the situation, and they were all, in their various ways, men who understood when words had reached the limit of their usefulness.

Antoine looked at the floor. He thought about a box with a brass clasp. He thought about a letter in his grandmother's hand, folded small, sitting in the dark of a hold that smelled of salt pork and four dead men.

He thought about what she had written at the bottom, underlined three times, that he had read and had not understood and was beginning, now, to understand.

"Tonight," he said.

Moreau nodded.

That was all.

Chapter Eleven

The Letter

He went at the last of the evening light, as Moreau had said. Before the second watch bell, while the passage still held something that could be called illumination rather than darkness with lantern holes punched in it. He took two lanterns — one in each hand, because he was not going into that hold with a single point of failure between himself and blindness — and he went alone, because Moreau had been right about that too, and he had observed during their voyage that Moreau was generally right about things he said with finality.

At the top of the hold ladder, he stopped.

"Captain," he had said, an hour before, finding Moreau at the stern rail where the man seemed to go when he needed to think without being observed thinking. "The girl said to return the trunk. To me."

Moreau had looked at him for a long moment. "The girl," he said, "also talks to a demon she calls Robin. I am not running this ship on the navigational advice of an eight-year-old's imaginary friend."

"It's not imaginary."

"I know it's not imaginary," Moreau said, with the particular exhaustion of a man who has had his entire epistemology dismantled in a single evening and has not yet had time to construct a replacement. "That is not the point. The point is that I am not returning the trunk of Antoine de la Mothe Cadillac to Antoine de la Mothe Cadillac on the recommendation of the thing that killed four of my men. If it wants the trunk moved, it can move it itself." A pause. "Which I acknowledge it is probably capable of."

"Then it will," Antoine said. "And you'll have no warning of when."

Moreau's jaw tightened. "Get the letter. Get out. Touch nothing else."

So Antoine stood at the top of the hold ladder with two lanterns and touched nothing else was the instruction and he almost laughed, because touching nothing else required getting within arm's reach of a trunk that had been demonstrating for two weeks that it had opinions about who touched it and when, and the instruction was the kind of instruction that sounded reasonable from the outside and revealed its absurdity the moment you were the man holding the lanterns.

He went down.

The hold smelled different.

Not worse, not better — different in the same way a room smells different after something has happened in it that cannot be undone. He had heard men describe this quality in battlefield hospitals, in rooms where people had died badly, this alteration in the character of the air itself, as if the molecules had rearranged themselves around the event and declined to go back. He breathed through his mouth and held both lanterns up and looked at the trunk.

It was sitting exactly where it had been. Against the port wall. The brass clasp closed.

The four men had been removed, wrapped, and committed. What remained was a darkening of the planking that the bilge water would eventually address, and a smell that the bilge water would not, and the trunk, patient as it had always been patient, sitting in the circle of his lantern light like something that had been expecting him.

He crossed to it. Set one lantern on the nearest crate. Crouched down.

"I'm not here for trouble," he said, and immediately felt like a fool for said it, and then immediately felt that feeling was probably irrelevant given the circumstances.

He opened the trunk.

The grandmother's box was where it had always been, in the left-front quadrant, the carved symbols dark against dark wood. He lifted it out and set it on the planking beside him and looked at the clasp. Closed. He pressed his thumb against it and felt it seated, solid, the same way it had been seated every time he had pressed it down, and the same way it had been standing open every morning after.

He opened it.

The iron nails, bound with red thread. The vial of salt. The bone-handled knife. The rosary and the prayer book nestled together. And the paper, folded small in the bottom corner, his grandmother's handwriting visible through the fold on the outer face, cramped and precise and very dark, as if she had pressed hard.

He took it. Unfolding it carefully, the paper brittle at the creases with age.

He held it toward the lantern and began to read.

The first part he knew. The list of protections, the instructions for warding, the catalog of what the iron nails were for and how the salt was to be used and what the knife had been used for by the women before her and what he might need to use it for himself. He read it with the attention of a man reading a military dispatch in the field, absorbing each piece of information and filing it, moving to the next. This part he had seen, or most of it — he had read it in the dark of his berth weeks ago before he had fully understood what he was reading.

Then he came to the part he hadn't seen, because the paper was folded in quarters and the quarter he had read before was not all of it.

He unfolded it further.

The handwriting changed. Not the hand — still his grandmother's, the same cramped precision — but the quality of the pressure behind it. Whatever she had written first had been written with the careful deliberateness of someone composing instructions. What she had written in the remaining portion had been written by someone in a state that the composure only barely contained.

He held it closer to the lantern and read.

***

Antoine, if you are reading this in full, then you have accepted what I could not make your father accept and what I could not make myself say aloud in all the years I tried. So I will write it plainly.

The name de la Mothe Cadillac carries a distinction that has nothing to do with the patent of nobility your great-grandfather purchased, though he purchased it with money he should not have had and did not deserve. The distinction is older. The distinction is a bargain.

Your great-grandfather Édouard found the creature in 1623, in the ruins of a farmhouse near Gascony that had burned in a way that left the fieldstone foundation intact and everything else ash. He did not summon it. This is important, and it is the one thing that has always made me feel something adjacent to compassion for Édouard, who was in almost every other respect a man I would have been glad never to meet. He did not summon it. It was simply there, in the ash and the fieldstone, sitting the way it sits, and it looked at him and it spoke to him, and Édouard, who was a desperate man in the particular way of men who believe they deserve more than God has given them, listened.

What it told him was this: it was old. Older than the farmhouse, older than Gascony, older than France, older than the word for France. It had been walking the earth since the day a man named Jesus Christ had cast it and its kind from a man into a herd of swine, and the swine had run into the sea, and some of its kind had gone into the water with the swine, and some had scattered before they could be caught, and it was among those who scattered, and it had been walking alone since that day, and it was very tired of walking alone.

Its kind, it told Édouard, were called Legion. This was not a name so much as a description of what they had been before the casting out, and what they wished to be again. They were diminished individually. Scattered, they were merely dangerous. Reunited, they were something else entirely, something for which Édouard's language had no adequate word, and the creature told him this with a satisfaction that Édouard described in his own account as the satisfaction of a man who knows he was being offered something the other men could not refuse.

The bargain it offered was this...

Antoine stopped reading. He was aware of the hold around him, of the wood and the dark and the smell of the place. He was aware of the trunk, three feet from where he crouched. He was aware that the lantern was burning steadily and that nothing in the hold was moving.

He held the paper closer and continued.

In exchange for its assistance — and its assistance, Édouard's account made clear, was considerable, the kind of help that could transform a failing farm into a prosperous estate, that could open doors that remained closed to men of Édouard's actual standing, that could arrange the deaths of creditors and the forgiveness of debts and the favor of men with power — in exchange for all of this, the creature required suffering.

Not Édouard's suffering. This was the nature of the bargain, and this is the thing that made it a bargain Édouard could accept. Not his suffering. The suffering of others. For every act of providence the creature arranged for the de la Mothe family, another family would pay the cost. Crops that failed inexplicably. Children who sickened without cause. Men who made one decision wrong at a moment when the wrong decision was fatal. The creature was precise about this. It was not random cruelty — it was transfer. The fortune that belonged to others, redirected. Édouard's success was not created. It was taken.

Édouard agreed. He had a large appetite and a small conscience, and the creature had correctly identified him as the kind of man who could live with arithmetic of this kind.

This is what you carry, Antoine. This is the de la Mothe Cadillac distinction. Every generation of our family's success has been paid for in the suffering of families we will never know. The land your great-grandfather left to his son. The commission your grandfather received above men more qualified. The patent of nobility. The ear of ministers. The King's favor that has put you on this ship.

All of it paid for. None of it by us.

Antoine sat back on his heels. The lantern light was very steady. His hands were not.

He found the place on the page and kept reading, because stopping now would be worse than continuing.

The creature has remained attached to our family because the bargain was never fulfilled on its side. It was promised assistance in finding its scattered brethren, in working toward the restoration of Legion. In exchange for the suffering it harvests through us, it expected to be led toward reunion. Édouard never understood this clause. He thought he was buying a servant. He was buying a partner, and the partner's goal was never our prosperity. Our prosperity was the mechanism.

What it wants is what it has always wanted since the day the swine ran into the sea.

To be whole again.

To be Legion again.

And Antoine — this is the part your father could not hear, the part that made him call me a frightened old woman and walk away — the creature can be constrained. Not destroyed. Not expelled. Constrained.

The suffering it requires does not have to come from others.

This is what I spent thirty years learning, and what I am not certain I have enough years left to explain properly, so I will be as plain as I know how to be:

The bargain can be rewritten. If you take the suffering onto yourself — if you stand before it and offer your own name, your own fortune, your own legacy as the vessel for what it harvests — it will accept. It prefers the concentrated source to the scattered one. It is more efficient. And the creature, whatever else it is, is efficient.

If you accept this, here is what it will cost you.

Your name will become synonymous with misfortune. Every city, every settlement, every enterprise you build will carry the mark of it. You will succeed — the creature will still deliver what it delivers — but the success will always be shadowed. Men will distrust you. History will treat you poorly. The things you build will outlast you and will not remember you kindly.

Your children will not be touched. The families who would have suffered will be spared. The creature will take from you what it took from them, and it will be enough, because you are willing, and willing suffering is more potent than unwilling suffering, and the creature knows this.

But Antoine, hear me:

If you accept this bargain, you must accept it completely. No half-measures. No later negotiations. The creature does not renegotiate. And you must renounce it before it names you a second time, because after the second naming the offer closes and what remains is only what it has always been: a thing that is patient and hungry and working its way back toward Legion one piece at a time, and your family name attached to that work forever, without any constraint at all.

You have the nails. You have the salt. You have the knife, which was used by your great-great-grandmother in a ceremony I have described on the additional page, which you should find folded beneath this one.

Find the additional page, Antoine.

Do not lose the additional page. Your father stared into the family ledger for hours. I am not sure why, as the ledger held nothing but names, from what I could see. But I saw that he saw more, much more than I could. But what I do not know. But in time, it drove him mad.

I am sorry I could not say this to your face. I tried. You were so certain, then, that the world was rational. I did not want to be the one to take that from you.

But I am taking it now, because someone must, and I am dead, and dead women have the advantage of having nothing left to lose.

Your grandmother, Marguerite.

***

He sat in the hold of La Vigilante for a long time after he finished reading.

The lantern burned. The ship moved. Somewhere above him forty-odd souls were going about the business of surviving an Atlantic crossing, and below him the ballast groaned, and around him the dark was the dark of a place that had seen four men die and had not been changed by it in any way that mattered.

He found the additional page, folded beneath the first. He unfolded it. Read it. Read it again.

Then he folded both pages together, precisely as they had been folded, and placed them back in the box. He placed the box in the trunk. He closed the trunk. He pressed the clasp down and felt it seat, and he held his thumb there for three full seconds, and then he lifted his thumb.

The clasp stayed closed.

He picked up both lanterns and stood. His knees ached from crouching. His hands had stopped shaking somewhere in the middle of his grandmother's letter and had not resumed, which surprised him and which he decided to take as a kind of sign, though he was no longer certain he believed in signs in the way that he had believed in them before tonight.

He looked at the trunk.

"I'll tell him," He said. "When I'm ready."

He went up the ladder and into the passage and up to the deck, where the night was clear and cold and the stars were out in their thousands over the black Atlantic, indifferent and ancient and arranged in patterns that men had been told stories about for as long as men had been looking up.

He found Moreau at the stern rail, where he always was.

"Well?" Moreau said.

"She wrote it all down," Antoine said.

"And?"

Antoine looked at the stars. He thought about Édouard in the ruins of a farmhouse in Gascony, and a thing in the ash that had been walking alone since the day the swine ran into the sea. He thought about the families he had never met whose suffering had purchased everything he had and was and carried. He thought about his children, and about the city he intended to build at the straits, and about what his grandmother had said regarding the things he built and how history would treat him.

He thought about a bargain that could be rewritten, and what rewriting it would cost, and what not rewriting it would cost instead.

"We need to return the trunk," he said.

Moreau said nothing.

"Not for the creature," Antoine said. "For me. I need what's inside it." He looked at the captain. "And I need a priest."

Moreau studied him for a long moment in the starlight, and whatever he saw in Antoine's face made him look away first, which was not something he had done before in Antoine's experience.

"In the morning," Moreau said.

"In the morning," Antoine agreed.

He went below to his berth and lay on his cot and stared at the canvas ceiling and did not sleep, and sometime in the small hours he heard, or thought he heard, from somewhere deep in the ship's belly, the sound of a trunk lid rising and falling.

Rising and falling.

Patient as a tide.

Waiting to see what he would do next.

Chapter Twelve

The Shepherd's Secret

Father Lescaut had chosen the common area because it was the largest enclosed space on the ship that wasn't the hold, and because people needed walls around them when they were frightened. Open sky made frightened people feel small. Walls made them feel contained, which was not the same as safe but was close enough to function on.

He had been a priest for nineteen years, and he knew how to read a room, and what he read in this one was the particular quality of fear that follows an event which had destroyed available explanations. These were not people afraid of the dark, or of the sea, or of the crossing. Before him were people who had been afraid of those things yesterday and now rose this morning to discover that those anxieties were small, manageable fears; fears that belonged to a world that still operated on comprehensible principles.

That world had closed its doors sometime in the night.

So, he stood at the head of the common area with his back to the galley wall and his book in his hands, and he gave them what he had, which was his voice and the two thousand years of institution behind him. He watched their faces and measured what landed and what didn't.

"Do not be deceived. What we have encountered," he said, "is not beyond the power of God to address. Evil is not coequal with good. It is not an opposing force of equal strength. It is a diminishment, a corruption, a thing that exists only in the absence of what it corrupts. Light does not struggle against darkness. It simply ends it."

"It killed four men," said a voice from the back. Mercier's bunkmate, Antoine thought, a Norman sailor named Gros whose face had not found its way back to its natural expression since the hold. "I don't see how that's a diminished thing."

"The capacity for destruction is not the same as power," Lescaut said, with the steady patience of a man who had answered harder questions in more hostile rooms. "A fire destroys. We do not, therefore, worship fire." He looked around the assembled faces — twenty, perhaps twenty-five, the ones who had come because they needed something to hold on to, and the priest was the best available option. "What we face has a name, and it has a history, and it has constraints. Monsieur Cadillac is working to understand these constraints. In the meantime, I want you to know that the sacraments are available to all of you. Confession. The Eucharist. These are not—"

"Can you exorcise it?" The question came from a woman near the front, one of the settler families, her hands folded in her lap with a tightness that suggested they had been folded that way for some hours. "A proper exorcism. The Rituale Romanum. Can you cast it out?"

The room focused. This was what they had come for, or part of it, the hope that the institution had a specific tool for this specific problem, that somewhere in the accumulated machinery of the Church there was a lever that addressed exactly this situation.

Lescaut took a breath. "The rite of exorcism is a powerful instrument of the Church's authority," he said. "I will not pretend otherwise. The power of Christ has prevailed against demonic forces since—"

He felt the small hand close around his wrist.

It arrived without warning, the way lightning arrives — not the thing itself but the sudden total whiteness of it, the obliteration of the present moment by something that was not the present moment.

He was in the common area of La Vigilante, and then he was not.

What replaced it was a room in Lyon. Stone walls. A narrow window through which the afternoon light came in at the particular angle it came in during late summer, when the sun was low enough to clear the abbey's west wall but high enough to fall across the rope bed in a long warm stripe. He could feel the roughness of the wool blanket beneath his hands. He could smell the beeswax from the chapel two floors below, rising through the stones in the manner smells rose in old buildings, carrying the sacred into spaces where it had no business being.

Sister Agnès was beneath him.

Her habit was folded on the chair by the door, she had folded it carefully, as if the folding were a kind of reverence, as if order in that small thing might stand in for order in the larger one. Her dark hair was unpinned and spread across the pillow and her eyes were open and looking up at him with an expression that was equal parts want and terror, the two things wound together so completely that he had told himself, then and afterward and for three years running, that one could not be separated from the other, that the terror was not the thing she felt but merely the shadow of the thing she felt, cast by the wall they were dismantling together.

He had believed this. He had needed to believe it and so he had, with the focused conviction of a man who understood that his entire framework required a particular thing to be true.

Her breath against his throat. Her hands at his back. The moans of pleasure she made, low and involuntary, that he had replayed in the confessional dark of his own conscience more times than he could count, always arriving at the same place — the place where he told himself she had come to him willingly, which was true, and that the power between them had been equal, which it was not.

She had been twenty-three years old. He had been her confessor. He had known for six months before that afternoon what was in her face when she looked at him, and he had done nothing to address it except allow it to grow, tending it with small attentions and private conversations, with the particular intimacy that confession created and that he had not, he could see this now, in the white-lit merciless clarity of whatever the child's touch had opened: had not been innocent of exploiting.

The child had been born in March. A boy. Taken before Agnès had properly seen him, given to a family whose name she was not told. Agnès had been transferred to an abbey in Brittany, which was the Church's method of handling such things — efficient and without appeal. Her name had not been spoken in Lyon again in his presence, and he had not spoken it, and he had received no censure beyond a private conversation with his superior that had resulted in a transfer of his own, to a different parish, a different city, a begin anew with a clean page.

Agnès had received the shame.

He had received the clean page.

He had told himself, for three years, that this was not his doing, that the institution had acted on its own logic, that he had not asked for the disparity.

But this was not true.

It simply was the most convenient truth available to him, and he had lived inside it with the comfort of a man who had found a house that fit him perfectly and had never asked why the previous tenant left.

He wrenched his wrist free.

The common area came back, all of it at once — the faces, the lanterns, the smell of too many people in too small a space — and Marguerite's tiny frame stood in front of him, her hand still extended from where he had pulled away from it, and her face was open and unguarded how children's faces are open when they have just looked through a window into a room they were not meant to see. Her hand covered her mouth. Her eyes were wide in surprise, disbelief, and shock.

She had seen it all.

Not just the afternoon in Lyon. The six months before it. The careful cultivation of what should have been protected. The child taken from a woman who had loved him, or had believed she loved him, which was the same thing at twenty-three. The clean page. The years of self-absolution dressed as contrition.

She had seen him as he was, stripped of the habit, decorum, learning and institutional authority. A hollow voice to falsity that had just told twenty people about the power of Christ over evil, and what she had seen was a man who had taken what he wanted from someone who trusted him and had paid nothing for it while she had paid everything.

The demon guiding the child had known exactly where to look to probe to elicit the exact action needed to dismantle faith among the priest's hearers.

Father Lescaut acted before he thought. His hand pushed her back — not violently, not with intent to harm, but with the force of a man closing a door against something he could not allow to be seen, a reflex as old as shame itself.

The child stumbled two steps. Caught herself. Looked at him with those eyes that had just seen Lyon.

"You're a bad man," she said.

The room was silent.

"Child—" he began.

"You pretend," she said, her chin beginning to tremble. "He says you all pretend." The tears were coming now, because she was eight years old and a priest had shoved her and the creature's gift had shown her things that eight-year-olds were not built to carry. "He says pretending is the only sin that doesn't know it's a sin."

She turned and ran.

The room watched her go. Then the room turned back to Father Lescaut.

The woman in the front row, the one who had asked for the Rituale Romanum, stood up slowly. She didn't look at Lescaut's face; she looked at his hand—the hand that had pushed a child. She pulled her shawl tight around her shoulders, a physical sealing-off of her spirit.

"She is a disturbed child," he said. His voice came out level. He was grateful, even now, for the training. "In contact with something that distorts and manipulates. What she says—"

"Father. We saw it too. Not just the child."

Bertrand. From the back. One word, carrying the weight of a man who had watched carefully and had made his own accounting.

Lescaut closed his book. The thud of the leather covers felt final, like a tomb door.

"I need to pray," he said. "I will be available for confession after the midday meal."

He moved toward the exit, but the room did not part gracefully this time. He had to shoulder his way through a thicket of cold shoulders and averted gazes. He felt the hem of his cassock brush against a passenger's boot, and the man pointedly drew his feet back, as if the fabric itself were contagious.

At the door, the child's voice drifted back from the passage, high and clear, cutting through the low, angry murmur rising behind him.

"He says your prayers bounce off the ceiling now," she called, not to him specifically, but to the air, to the room, to whoever was listening. The voice of a child delivering a message carefully, making sure she had it right. "He says when they fall back down they sound like someone else's name."

Lescaut didn't look back. He couldn't. Behind him, the common area was no longer a sanctuary but twenty pairs of eyes that now stood in judgment of the man of God.

The passage to his quarters was very long.

He locked the door behind him and knelt on the planking in the dark, and his hands found each other, his mouth opened, and the words came, because nineteen years had put them somewhere beneath conscious retrieval.

But somewhere in the third line of the Pater Noster he stopped.

Because Marguerite's voice was in his ears. And what was sitting in his chest was neither the prayer nor the shame, though both were present, but the specific and terrible clarity of a man who has spent three years building a scaffolding of self-justification and had just watched a child's hand take it apart in the space of a heartbeat.

Agnès was in Brittany. Her son was with a family whose name neither he nor she knew And he was on his knees in a ship's cabin in the North Atlantic, carrying the sacraments of the Church toward a wilderness settlement, with a creature from hell in the hold below him that had looked into the secret place of his soul where he kept concealed what he had done and had found it immediately, searching, in the same manner you find something in a room when you know exactly where it was left.

When they fall back down, they sound like someone else's name.

He remained kneeling for a very long time. The candle burned down on the shelf above him. Outside, the ship moved through the Atlantic with its usual indifference.

He struggled to speak to God, as he could no longer remember how to begin.

Chapter Thirteen

The Cost of the Name

They met in the captain's chart room because it was the most private space available that wasn't the hold or a man's personal berth, and privacy was what this conversation required. Moreau had vacated it without being asked, which told Antoine that the captain understood more about what was happening on his ship than he had let on, and had decided that his most useful contribution at this point was absence.

Father Lescaut was already there when Antoine arrived. He was sitting at the chart table with his hands flat on the surface in front of him, not holding anything, not reading anything. His face had recovered its color since the common area but not its composure, and Antoine decided that the lack of composure was more trustworthy than the recovery of color, so he sat down across from him and put his grandmother's letter on the table between them.

"Read it," he said.

Lescaut read it. He read it the way he had listened in the common area — with the complete attention of a man for whom information was a professional instrument. He did not change expression. When he finished, he refolded it along its original creases and placed it back on the table and looked at Antoine.

"Your great-grandfather made his bargain in 1623," he said.

"According to her account," said Antoine.

"And in all the generations since, no one has attempted to renegotiate?" said the father.

"My grandmother discovered it was possible. She had spent thirty years learning how." Antoine looked at the letter. "But my father wouldn't hear it. He called her a frightened old woman, and she let him believe that because the alternative was to tell him what the family's success had cost, and he was—" he stopped. "He was a man who very much liked his success."

Lescaut was quiet for a moment. Outside the chart room the ship made its sounds, the ordinary sounds that had become in the last weeks a kind of taunt, the normalcy of timber and water pretending nothing was wrong below decks.

"The church has seen this before," Lescaut said.

Antoine looked at him.

"Not this specific situation. Not the Nain Rouge by name." Lescaut's hands moved slightly on the table, a small, controlled gesture. "In Brittany. A fishing family. Three generations of unusual fortune, boats that returned when others sank, catches that defied the season. And around them, at a consistent radius, families who suffered in ways that had no natural explanation." He paused. "The Church and thus those she discipled called it coincidence. I was twenty-six and newly ordained, and I called it coincidence too, because that was what I had been trained to call it."

Another pause, longer.

"The family patriarch died with his eyes open, looking at something in the corner of the room that no one else could see. He was smiling."

"He was relieved," Antoine said.

"Yes. I think that's right." Lescaut looked at him steadily. "I think he had been waiting for it to be finished."

Antoine put his hands on the table beside the letter. He looked at them, the hands that had signed his commission papers, that had shaken the hand of Minister Pontchartrain, that had held the silver compass and felt the wrongness in it and told himself it was the case warping. "What does she mean by the ritual," he said. "The additional page. She describes a ceremony, but she doesn't—" he stopped. "She says the knife and the nails and the salt. She says I'll understand when I read the instructions. I've read them three times and I'm not certain I understand."

Lescaut was quiet for a moment. Then he reached across and turned the additional page toward him and read it again, slowly, his lips moving slightly.

"I understand it," he said.

Antoine looked at him curiously. "Tell me."

Father Lescaut looked up. "The iron nail through the palm," he said, without preamble, because the conversation had moved past the point where preamble served any function. "Not a scratch. Not a cut, but through. The salt packed into the wound while it is open." He held Antoine's gaze. "This is not metaphor. It is not symbolic. Your grandmother was precise about this because the ceremony requires the precision. The pain has to be real. The blood has to be real. The body has to know the cost before the mouth says the words."

Antoine said nothing.

"And the words," Lescaut continued, "are the part that makes the nail bearable by comparison. Because Antoine—" he said the name with the weight of a man who understands he was speaking to someone whose relationship with that name was about to become very complicated "—the renunciation your grandmother describes is not a renunciation of Satan in the conventional sense. It is specific. It is surgical." He placed his finger on a line of the additional page. "You must renounce your name. Not as a spiritual abstraction. Specifically. The name de la Mothe Cadillac and everything it has purchased. The commission. The patent of nobility. The favor of ministers. The ear of the King." He looked up again. "Everything the creature's work has given you. To free yourself from ghosts of the lives taken to build your house — for fraternizing with the devil. You must give it back."

"Give it back to whom?"

"That is the question your grandmother does not answer, which I suspect is intentional." Lescaut sat back. "I think the giving back is the act itself. The renunciation. Whether it is received by anyone in particular may be less important than the willingness to release it."

Antoine looked at the letter, and his brow furrowed.

"The city," he said. "I am going to build a city at the straits. I have the King's commission. Men aboard this vessel who have come because I promised them land grants and futures." He looked up. "If I renounce the name, if I renounce everything the creature purchased — what does that do to the city? What does that do to them?"

Lescaut was quiet for a moment.

"Your grandmother says the creature will still deliver," he said carefully. "The terms change, but the capacity remains. What changes is the source of the cost. You, not others. Your name will carry the shadow. It appears that your legacy will be..."

He searched for the word. "...contested. History will not treat you simply."

"I know," Antoine said. "She told me."

"But the city itself..." Lescaut paused, choosing his words with the care of a man who understood their weight, "...the city may survive you better than you survive it. That may be the nature of the transfer. You carry the mark. The thing you build carries only itself."

Antoine sat with this for a moment that stretched longer than it should have.

"There is something else," Lescaut said. His voice had changed slightly; taken on the quality it had in the common area when he was giving people something they needed to hold on to. Except now there was nothing of performance in it. It was the voice of a man who has information and is deciding how much of it serves the listener. "Based on what your grandmother writes about the creature's nature. About Legion."

"Tell me."

"If what she describes is accurate — if this is genuinely one of the entities cast out at Gadarene, then everyone on this ship is in more danger than four dead men suggests." He said it flatly, without drama, because drama would have made it smaller. "The entity she describes is not satisfied with individual harvest. It is working toward something. And a ship at sea..." he looked at the wall, beyond which the Atlantic continued its indifferent business, "...is a closed system. If it decides that its patience has run out, that it no longer needs to manage the situation gradually..."

"It could take the ship," Antoine said.

"It could take the ship," Lescaut confirmed. "Every soul aboard. And it would not need to be gradual about it."

Antoine opened his mouth.

From above them, through the deck planking, through the timbers, through every layer of wood between the chart room and the open air, came a sound that arrived in the chest before the ears processed it — high and ragged and suddenly cut off, the sound of a man's voice doing something that a man's voice was not designed to do.

Then shouting. Multiple voices. The sound of running feet.

They raced up the ladder before either of them had decided to move.

* * *

The deck was lit by the last of the evening light, that flat Atlantic dusk that flattened everything and cast no shadows worth the name, and in it the crew had gathered at the mainmast in the posture of people surrounding an event they could not look away from and yet could not look at.

Antoine pushed through.

The man's name was Gilles, a rigger from Normandy who had been working the upper lines, and he had come down in the way that men come down when they haven't chosen to come down — the rope that should have been in his hand had taken a different relationship with his body, and found his neck in the manner ropes find necks when the geometry of a fall goes wrong, and he hung at the height of a man's shoulder, still, with the specific stillness of something that had recently been moving and would not move again.

Charbonneau had his knife out already. Two other men were taking the weight. Antoine got his hands on the rope, and they brought Gilles down to the deck, and Father Lescaut was there immediately, kneeling, his fingers at the man's throat.

A long moment.

"He's alive," Lescaut said. "Get him below. On his side."

The crew moved. Antoine stood and looked at the mast and the rope, and the geometry of what had happened, and none of it made sense. The man's foot found a wrong place, and there was nothing logical of the entanglement. The rope had not been in a position to do what it had done. The angle was wrong. The rope had gone where ropes did not go without assistance.

"Monsieur Cadillac." Spoke a child's voice.

He turned.

Marguerite was at the rail. She was wearing her traveling cloak, which struck him as strange, as if she had dressed for weather or for some event she had been told to prepare for. Her hands were folded in front of her and her face wore its expression, the waiting one, the one that had been waiting since La Rochelle.

"It's almost night," she said.

Antoine looked at the horizon. The sun was at the waterline, balanced there, the last of it.

"I know," he said.

"He says you know what needs to be done." She tilted her head. "He says the trunk is still in the wrong place." She looked at him with that expression that was not a child's expression and had not been, he now understood, since the dock at La Rochelle. "He says he has been patient. He says patience is a choice he makes." A pause. "He says he can make other choices."

Father Lescaut came to stand beside Antoine. He looked at the girl, then at the horizon, and then at Antoine.

"Tonight," he said quietly. "It has to be tonight."

Antoine looked at Marguerite. And she returned his gaze.

"Tell him," Antoine said, "that I'll need until after the second watch bell."

Marguerite was quiet for a moment, her head tilted, listening to something they couldn't hear.

Then she nodded.

"He says that is acceptable," she said. "He says to bring the priest." She paused, and something moved across her face that was not her expression, that belonged to something older and more patient than an eight-year-old. "He says Father Lescaut already knows the words. He just needs to remember that he's allowed to say them."

She turned and walked back toward the hatch, unhurried, as if the evening were completely ordinary and she had simply been relaying a message, which was, as Antoine supposed, exactly what she had been doing.

The sun went below the waterline.

And darkness encroached across the sky to settle into position.

Chapter Fourteen

The Renewal of the Pact

Antoine and Father Lescaut went down into the hold together at the second watch bell, as agreed.

Lescaut carried a lantern, his stole and the small leather case that contained what remained of his sacramental kit after the crossing, a vial of holy water, the crucifix on its chain, the ritual book whose pages he had spent the last two hours reviewing with the focused attention of a man preparing for an examination he could not afford to fail. He had heard Antoine's confession in the chart room before they descended. A full confession. The first complete accounting Antoine had given to God or man of what his family carried and what he himself had done and failed to do, and Lescaut had listened to all of it without flinching and had given absolution with the full weight of his authority and his intention, and when Antoine had looked at him afterward with something that might have been surprise Lescaut had said only:

"I am not a good man. But I am still a priest, a representative of God and of his Church. Those are not the same things, and tonight the second one is what matters."

He meant it. And a confession by Father Lescaut to Antoine was not expected — that after everything the creature had shown the man through Marguerite's touch, after the exposure in the common area and the hours alone in his cabin unable to begin, Lescaut had arrived at the chart room composed and purposeful and genuinely, unmistakably resolved. Not performing resolution. Not wearing it out of fear. Resolved how men become resolved when they have examined their sins completely and have decided that the examination is finished and the work is what remains. He had made his peace with God.

He had chosen to be a priest tonight.

Whatever else he was, he had chosen that.

Antoine carried his grandmother's box. He had repacked it in the hold after reading the letter, the nails, the salt, the knife, the additional page folded precisely as his grandmother had folded it, and he carried it now under his arm with the careful ambivalence of a man carrying something he has decided not to have feelings about. He had been very good at this for a long time, and he was good at it now.

The hold received them with its smell.

Lescaut set the lantern on the provision crate and opened his ritual book and kissed his stole and placed it around his neck with the deliberateness of a man putting on armor. He looked at Antoine.

"Are you ready?"

"Yes," Antoine said.

This was not entirely true, but it was true enough to function on, and Father Lescaut accepted it in the manner he had accepted everything Antoine had told him in the last several hours, completely, without editorial, storing it for later consideration that would not happen until after the work was done.

"Then let us begin."

He opened the book to the place he had marked and began to read.

The Latin came out of him with the authority of a man who had spoken it ten thousand times in circumstances ranging from the mundane to the genuine, the authority of repetition, yes, but also something underneath the repetition, something that the repetition had worn smooth and revealed, like water wears stone smooth and reveals the grain of what was always there. His voice was steady. His hands were steady. The lantern light fell on the page and his face and the trunk against the port wall and the place on the planking that was still darker than the planking around it.

The temperature dropped.

Not dramatically. Not the theatrical plummet of penny-novel hauntings. Just a degree, two degrees, the kind of change you felt in your hands first, then in the fine hairs on the back of your wrists, in the same way your next breath fogged slightly in the lantern light where your previous breath had not.

Lescaut continued reading.

The shadows in the hold changed quality. This was the only way Antoine could describe it afterward: they did not move, did not deepen, did not reach or stretch. They just changed quality, like the quality of silence changes when someone has entered the room and has not yet spoken. The shadows became inhabited.

Lescaut turned a page. His voice did not waver.

"Exorcizo te, omnis spiritus immunde, in nomine Dei Patris omnipotentis—"

An animal like growl could be heard and the veil between the invisible and the visible strained to maintain their bounds. And a figure began to appear.

Not emerging. Not materializing. Simply present — as if it had always been there and had merely allowed itself to be seen. It stood in the space between the provision stacks and the port hull, no taller than a child's hip, draped in a red coat that moved like shadow, and its eyes were as the red of coals and its grin was the grin of something that has been waiting for an appointment it scheduled a long time ago and was pleased to see everyone had arrived on time.

It looked at Antoine first.

The look was warm. That was the horror of it: genuinely warm, like an old acquaintance is greeted, much as someone is warm with you when they have known you longer than you have known yourself and found the knowing affectionate rather than contemptuous. It looked at Antoine the way a creditor looked at a debtor who had finally, after long delay, come to the window.

"Antoine," it said. The voice was the child's voice, always the child's voice, high and precise. "I wondered when you would come."

Antoine realized in that moment that he had just been named once.
"I came," Antoine said.

"We both knew you could not avoid this forever." The demon's words were not a reproach but an observation, delivered with something that was almost sympathy. It continued, "None of them can. They try. Your grandfather tried for eleven years. Your father — well, he was cleverer. He told himself the pact wasn't real and nearly made himself believe it, right up until the end." The red eyes moved across Antoine's face with the affectionate attention of a portrait painter.

"But you. You've known since La Rochelle. Since before La Rochelle, if you're honest. Since the night you were seventeen and you looked across a Paris dining room and saw your father's face when my name came up in conversation, and you understood something had happened to him that he would never explain."

Antoine said nothing.

"It's all right," the creature said, and it meant it, and that was the worst thing. It genuinely meant it.

"It will be all right. It always is, in the end. All I require is blood. The Creator himself demands it, you know, and so we mimic his example in search of means to restore to us what the Priest's God has taken." It tilted its head, those burning eyes going somewhere distant and then returned. "The life of the flesh is in the blood. He said that. Not me. I have merely always agreed with him on that particular point."

Lescaut had stopped reading.

He was looking at the creature with the expression of a man who has spent his professional life studying a subject and had just encountered the primary source, not fear exactly, though fear was present, but something more complicated, the specific unease of a theologian confronting a thing that knew the biblical texts and was not wrong about them.

"What are you talking about?" Lescaut said. His voice was level. The training holding. "Blood for what?"

The creature's grin widened by a precise degree. "Ask him," it said. "He knows."

Lescaut looked at Antoine.

Antoine looked at the creature. "Get on with it," he said, to the priest. "The ritual."

Lescaut held his gaze for a moment. Then he looked back at his book and found his place, and continued.

The ritual proceeded.

It was not like the stories. It was not like the illustrated broadsides, or the whispered accounts, or the theatrical performances that had made the Rituale Romanum into something half legend. It was methodical and careful and, in many ways, mundane, in the same way all serious work is mundane in its execution regardless of its stakes. The priest moved through each section of the rite with the focused precision of a surgeon, the words building on each other with the accumulated weight of two thousand years of institutional authority, the holy water falling in precise drops, the crucifix held forward with a steadiness that cost Lescaut something but cost him willingly.

The creature watched. It did not flinch from the holy water. It did not recoil from the crucifix. It stood in its red coat and watched the ritual with the attentive patience of a thing that had seen this done before and knew how it would end and was curious, genuinely curious, about whether this time would be different.

Because this time, as before...*might* be different.

Antoine could see it in the creature's eyes, the recognition that this priest, compromised as he was, had despite his flaws brought something genuine to the hold. The authority Lescaut carried was not diminished by his sin. The Church's power did not operate through the moral perfection of its instruments. The demon knew this. The Church had always known this. The distinction between the sacrament and the sinner administering it was two thousand years old, and the creature had lived through all two thousand of those years and had watched the Church use that distinction as both shield and sword, and tonight it was a shield, and the creature was not entirely comfortable with it.

It was compellable and its discomfort could be discerned, and its malevolence toward the father became increasing palpable.

That was the truth in the hold. If Antoine renounced, the creature was compellable. The priest had the authority, and the words were the words. The creature could not simply choose not to be bound by them. For in the economy of Christ, every knee must bow.

And Antoine discerned it was waiting to see if Antoine would give the priest the chance to use them.

Antoine watched the ritual and felt the weight of the grandmother's box under his arm and thought about the ledger with its names going back to Édouard, and thought about Detroit, and thought about the commission in his trunk, and thought about the faces of the passengers at the committal of four men they hadn't known, and thought about Céleste holding her daughter's hand and asking him if everything was going to be all right, and he had told her yes.

He thought about the letter in his coat, pressed against his ribs.

He thought about his grandmother Marguerite, who had spent thirty years learning what he needed to know and had died with the box latched and the knowledge in it and her faith that he would eventually be ready to do what must be done to be rid of the Nain Rouge.

He thought about the city.

The ritual reached the renunciation.

Lescaut looked up from the book. His eyes found Antoine's. He gave a slight nod — *here*, the nod said, *this moment is what everything has been building toward, say the words and it is done, I am here; I have the authority, say the words.*

His face in the lantern light was the face of a man who had chosen tonight to be a priest. Who had heard a confession and meant the absolution. Who had descended into a hold that smelled of four dead men to stand between a colonial commandant and an entity that had been walking the earth since before the day the swine ran into the water and had done it not because he was unafraid but because he had decided that his fear was not the relevant consideration.

Father Lescaut was, Antoine thought, the best version of himself tonight. Perhaps the only time in his life he had been the best version of himself.

Antoine opened his mouth.

And paused.

The pause lasted four seconds. Perhaps five. The kind of pause that is not hesitation but decision — not the pause of a man who doesn't know what to say but the pause of a man who knows exactly what he is about to choose and is allowing himself one final moment of full awareness before the choice becomes irrevocable.

Father Lescaut waited. His face did not change. He was a priest, and priests waited.

The creature waited too. But *its* expression had now changed.

It was watching Antoine with the expression it had worn when it looked at the compass sitting wrong in Moreau's pocket — the expression of something that has made a prediction and is watching the prediction confirm itself. Not triumphant. Not gloating. Simply the expression of something ancient that has seen this moment before, with this exact quality of silence, and knew with the certainty of long experience what came next. To know that there was nothing new under the sun.

"Ah," it said softly.

Just that.

A sound less like a word than like a door closing somewhere.

It looked at Lescaut. Then looked back at Antoine. Then at Lescaut again.

"Do you know, priest, I saw the same thing with his father, and with his grandfather before him." Its voice had gone soft, contemplative, the voice of something reviewing a long history with a kind of melancholy that sounded almost genuine.

"They stand there, exactly as he is standing now, and they open their mouths, and I watch their faces, and I always know." The demon tilted its head. And the grinning red imp turned to look at Lescaut. "Would you like to know how I know?"

Lescaut did not respond. He was looking at Antoine.

"The eyes," the creature said. "It's not what they look at. It's what they stop looking at."

A pause.

"His grandfather stopped looking at his wife's face. His father, well he stopped looking at the window, he could see the Paris street from where he stood and the children that were on it, and he stopped looking at them." Those demonic red eyes then moved to Antoine with something that was, horribly, almost gentle.

"Antoine here...well, he stopped looking at you, Father. A moment ago, he was looking at you. Now he is not. He is looking somewhere else. Somewhere only he can see."

Father Lescaut turned to Antoine fully.

"Antoine," he said. Quietly. "What is it talking about? What are you looking at?"

Antoine said nothing.

"Don't you know?" The creature said, surprised. "He is looking at Detroit, Father."

The hold was very quiet.

The Nain Rouge continued, "I have never blamed them," the creature said, and there was something in its voice that was the furthest thing from blame, an ancient, patient, almost fond resignation. "His forefathers have stood in this moment, and I have asked them some variance of the same question I will ask him now."

It looked directly at Antoine, the red eyes unwavering, and its voice when it spoke was soft as a confessor's.

"How many will you let die to build your city?"

What Antoine said next, he said quietly. Without drama. Without the theatrical weight of a man making a declaration. He said it as he said everything important, in the register of a man giving an administrative report, clear, precise and final.

"As many as you desire," he said. "Except as needed to bring the ship to port."

The Nain Rouge smiled, "Then it is settled, *Antoine de la Mothe Cadillac*, please update the ledger." And the silence that followed was absolute.

Father Lescaut stood with his ritual book open in his hands and his stole around his neck and his crucifix extended and his holy water spent and his genuine, hard-won, costly authority fully assembled and ready and entirely useless now, because the power of the rite ran through the man who stood beside him and the man who stood beside him had just spoken, and what he had spoken was not renunciation but endorsement. Cold, calculated approval.

He looked at Antoine.

Antoine met his eyes. Held them and did not look away.

There was no shame in Antoine's face. Perhaps briefly, in the space of that four-second pause, Father Lescaut believed he had seen it, genuine and complete, a flash of it, the real thing, and then it had passed, and what remained was the face of a man who has made his calculation and found it satisfactory and was done with the part of the process that involved feelings.

Lescaut understood then what the creature had said in the common area, on the other side of Marguerite's small hand, through the images it had given him. It had shown him his own sin to prepare him for this moment. To make sure he was paying attention when it mattered. To ensure he recognized what he was looking at when Antoine de la Mothe Cadillac, Commandant of the expedition to found Fort Pontchartrain du Détroit, looked at a hold full of authority assembled on his behalf and chose his family's blood ledger instead.

"Selfishness and pride," the creature said, grinning. Its voice was warm with a delight so genuine it was almost innocent. "After all this time. After everything. Still selfishness and pride." It looked between the two men with the expression of something that has just received exactly what it wanted and was taking a moment to appreciate it fully. "I love it," it said. "I genuinely love it."

"Antoine," Lescaut's voice had changed. The pastoral warmth was gone from it. What remained was something harder: the voice of a man who had been standing in a room and had now understood what the room actually was. "What you have just said. Do you understand what you have just—"

"Yes," Antoine said.

"Those are people. The passengers. The crew. They have—"

"Yes," Antoine said again. The same word. The same tone. Final.

Father Lescaut looked at him for a long time. Long enough that the creature's patience was the most dignified thing in the hold.

Lescaut then closed his ritual book.

The sound of it snapping shut was small in the hold's silence. A minuscule last sound. The sound of something that had been possible and was no longer possible, like the door of something swinging shut.

He removed his stole from around his neck. He folded it with the automatic reverence of long habit and held it in his hands and looked at it and then looked at Antoine.

"You are beyond my help," he said. "Not beyond God's. But beyond mine."

"I know," Antoine said. "I'm sorry."

"No," Lescaut said. "You are not."

He was right. Antoine looked at him and knew he was right and had nothing to say about it.

The creature watched this exchange with the attentive pleasure of a theatergoer watching a play it has seen before and loves particularly well. It had been right about the eyes. It was always right about the eyes.

What happened next happened quickly.

Antoine moved. The priest did not see it coming as he was looking at Antoine's face, at the eyes that had stopped looking at him, and he was thinking about Agnes in a room in Lyon and the child taken before she had properly seen him, thinking about clean pages and what they cost, and the nail was in Antoine's hand from the grandmother's box and it was in motion before Lescaut's peripheral vision had resolved the movement into something his body could respond to.

The iron nail drove through the center of Lescaut's palm.

The scream that came out of him was not a word. Nor a prayer. It was the pure unrehearsed sound of a body receiving something it was not prepared to receive — high, ragged and brief, because Lescaut was a man of discipline and the discipline reasserted itself almost immediately, and what replaced the scream was a sustained low sound, the sound of a man holding something back by force of sheer will because the alternative was to lose himself entirely to the pain.

He looked at his hand. At the nail. At the blood.

He looked at Antoine.

Antoine met his eyes.

The blood dripped from Lescaut's palm onto the planking and the creature inhaled, not through a nose, not through any visible aperture, but the inhalation was real and audible, and the hold seemed to draw inward slightly, like a room inhaling, like the ship's hold recognized the renewal of something it had been waiting to receive.

The pact was now enforced for another generation. The blood was real. The blood of a genuine man of God, spilled in the belly of the ship, by the hand of the man who had stood in the place of renunciation and had instead chosen himself.

The creature looked at Antoine with the expression of a parent watching a child accomplish something difficult.

"I knew you could do it," it said.

The creature then turned its attention to Lescaut.

It looked at him the way it had looked at everything on this ship, with complete attention, with the focused patience of something that had all the time it needed and intended to use exactly as much of it as the moment deserved. It looked at him how a surgeon looks at a patient, or like a confessor looks at a penitent, with the particular intimacy of something that knows you completely and has known you longer than you have known yourself.

Never let the Rouge name you twice.

I am sorry, grandmother.

Antoine watched as the demon he had unleashed sauntered towards the man of God.

* * *

It knew what Lescaut carried. It had put its knowledge through Marguerite's hand and shown him to himself, and it knew the shape of the sin and the shape of the man who had built a life around not being accountable for it. The woman in Lyon. The child taken before she had seen his face. The clean page. The years of liturgy spoken over an interior that had never been examined because examination would have required a reckoning that was easier to defer. But the demon knew the ceremony could not be performed while the sin was hidden. So, the confessor must confess. Thus, the creature forced the father to face his own sin. To humble him that he might confess his sin to God. To receive what his kind could not. Absolution. And in doing so, provide himself and Heaven a true witness of the pacts continuance or end. After all, he did the priest a favor, as he would be with God soon.

The demon was not angry. It was never angry. Anger was for creatures with something at stake in the outcome. It had nothing at stake. It simply proceeded with the particular relish of something that found its work satisfying. He walked towards the priest as a predator stalks its prey. Its red eyes glowed with contempt for this man of dirt and clay. And with those thoughts; he began to perform his own ritual. To recite the words of Christ.

"If thy right eye offend thee," it said, "pluck it out."

The Nain Rouge quoted Christ with the precision of a scholar and the pleasure of something that had been present when the words were first spoken and had been waiting ever since for the right opportunity to return them to a servant of God.

Lescaut understood. He was an intelligent man, and he understood the citation and its intended application, and he looked at the creature, and he summoned courage and did not run. He stood with his stole in one hand and the nail through the other, and he chose, in the last moment available to him for choosing, not to run.

He closed his eyes, and prayed. Not Latin. Not the ritual. Just words, the words of a man talking directly to the God he had been performing for nineteen years without speaking to plainly, and perhaps the plainness was too late and perhaps it was not, but he spoke it anyway because the alternative was silence and he was done with the things he had chosen out of convenience.

The creature moved toward him.

One could describe what it did next as theological. Not random cruelty, not the expression of appetite, but something that had been designed with the precision of a punishment that fit its specific crime. An administration of the ancient law of sowing and reaping. Lescaut had used his body as an instrument of betrayal. He had used the authority of his office as cover for what his lust wanted. And let another person pay the cost of what his body had done while his body went on to the next parish, the next pulpit, the next congregation of people who needed something real and received his performance instead.

The creature took from him what he had used as a weapon.

It was not quick. It was thorough.

And it quoted scripture throughout its disembowelment.

Lescaut screamed. The screaming was brief, not because the creature was merciful, but because a man can only sustain that register of sound for so long before the body overrides the voice. What replaced the screaming was worse in its way, the sounds of a man still present in his suffering, still conscious, still the intelligent man he had always been, understanding with complete clarity what was being done to him and why, and what said understanding cost him.

The creature ate what it took. Deliberately. In front of him. With the solemn attention of someone performing a sacrament, it finished. It stood in the hold, and it looked at what remained of Father Lescaut, who had come down into this hold tonight as the best version of himself. A man of God brought into the bowels of a ship to serve as a sacrifice to continue the benefits bestowed upon his family. And Antonie? He was a man who had brought him here and who was standing now with his back to all of it, face to the forward hull, breathing.

When the sounds stopped he did not turn around immediately.

The creature turned after its kill and looked at Antoine's back.

He waited until the hold was quiet. Then he turned.

He looked at what remained of Father Lescaut for one moment. Acknowledging the creature then he went to the trunk and opened it, and took out the family's ledger. The footsteps of the demon were heard from his rear as it ascended from the hold.

Antoine sat on the provision crate with the ledger in his lap and opened it to the first page, and he read the name at the top, which was a name he did not know: The farming family in Gascony, 1624. The fisherman's family near Bordeaux, 1631, and he turned the page, and there were more names, and he turned more pages, and there were always more names.

From above, through the planking, through the timbers, through the dark between decks, the screaming started.

He turned another page.

The names accumulated through the pages the way names accumulate in parish records, in the rolls of the dead, in the administrative documents of catastrophe — steadily, at first without drama, each one a life and a family and a future that had been redirected into the de la Mothe account without their knowledge or consent. Slowly, as if a veil were removed from the ledger's pages, he could see images, pictures...memories. And with each turning, he understood why his grandmother had warned him of his father's madness. For with each entry, an image, a visage, was given him of the person and or family whose fortunes were snuffed to secure his. He was given a panoramic display in his mind...connected by whatever enchantment the Nain Rouge held over the book of what it took. In each entry.... and there were hundreds dating back several generations; he saw the faces, the destruction of crops, the miscarriages both of fetus and justice taken from one family and transferred to his own to secure his family name. Image after haunting image assaulted him. And now he understood the fullness of the Nain Rouge's price. The irony of the demon that he had entered into covenant. For as Christ took upon himself the suffering of the world. Antoine would now see the suffering his family had inflicted. He would in the night hours see how his transactions elevated him above other men.

His mind reeled as the books, names, and visions seeped into his consciousness. What his grandmother saw as mere names, Antoine could see the sin listed, the transaction cost, invisible to all but he with whom the covenant was made. *He* would know. And would not be allowed to forget. As the ledger's history assaulted him, he saw that even his own grandmother was the result of the Rouge killing her intended. A man who had mysteriously died. Next to his name, the word "Covetousness" was written. The sin committed to secure his grandfather's beautiful prize. His grandfather, a man conveniently positioned to comfort and marry the woman he secretly lusted after. Antoine saw the memories in the ledger, and it showed him the curiosity in his grandmother's eyes when she herself saw her old fiancé's name in the family's ledger. The awareness, the horror, knowing that her progeny resulted from demonic intervention. And she despised her grandfather from that day forth and set herself to understand the pact that underlaid the Cadillac name.

Story after story flooded him.

Sin after sin.

All a debt inscribed in the old leather family ledger.

Antoine turned a page as the echoes of screams descended from above.

The names continued.

He did not go up.

Chapter Fifteen

The Captain's Last Stand

Captain Moreau knew something had changed before he had words for what it was.

He was at his chart table when it happened, not charting, not calculating, simply sitting in the way that men sit when they are waiting for something they cannot name and have been waiting long enough that the waiting has become its own kind of work. He had sent Renard to check on the hold watch an hour ago and Renard had not come back, and the quality of the sounds coming through the ship's timbers had been changing in ways that his thirty years of reading ships told him had nothing to do with weather or sea state or the ordinary complaints of a working vessel.

The compass on his table spun.

Not the slow drift of a needle responding to interference: the full rotation of something being driven, the brass face a blur, the click of the pivot going too fast to distinguish individual beats, the whole instrument chattering against the table with a sound like a playing card in bicycle spokes, faster and faster until the compass was not a navigational instrument anymore but simply a thing that had been taken over by a force that had no interest in north.

Moreau put his hand on it. The spinning continued through his palm; the case vibrating against his skin with a frequency that moved up his arm and into his teeth.

He took his hand away, then looked at the wall.

The wall of his cabin was bleeding.

Not pouring, no, nothing so dramatic. Just seeping, as old stone seeps in wet weather, finding the grain of the timber and running down it in dark, slow threads, following the wood's own channels, the blood patient and deliberate and almost black in the lantern light. It came from everywhere and nowhere, from the wood itself, as if the ship had been holding it and had determined to hold it no longer. It ran down the walls in lines that followed the grain and pooled alongside the baseboards and found its way across the floor toward his boots with the unhurried certainty of something that had all the time in the world.

Moreau looked at his boots and watched the blood reach them and embracing the leather and lurking to find its way around the sole.

He stood up and went to his sea chest and removed the second pistol. He had loaded both that morning, not knowing why, the action of a man whose body understood something his mind was still catching up to — and he checked the prime on both and set them on the chart table beside the spinning compass and stood with his back to the far wall and faced the door.

Above him, the deck was coming apart as a human community.

* * *

It had begun with the rigging.

Bertrand was the first man taken. He had been at the mainmast checking a line that had been giving him trouble since the storm, his hands moving through the familiar work with the automatic competence of thirty years, and the line had moved on its own. Not the movement of a line in wind — wind moved rope in arcs, in lateral swings, in the predictable physics of tension and release. This was different. This was a line moving with intent, finding Bertrand's wrists with the focused precision of something that knew exactly what it was doing, and before he had fully registered what was happening, he was lifted into the air.

Inverted. Four feet off the deck. His arms extended above him; below him, his face turned down toward the planking, his blood going to his head, the rigging held him in a configuration that required multiple points of tension all working in coordination, all holding at exactly the right angles, as if the ship's entire rope system had reorganized itself around the project of suspending this one man in this one position.

He was not alone.

Along the deck, in the time it took Bertrand to be lifted, four other men were taken the same way. Slowly the rigging worked through each of them with unhurried precision, finding wrists, ankles and throats, lifting each man and inverting them suspended at heights ranging from knee-level to mast-height, each one in a different configuration, as if something were working through the possibilities with the patient curiosity of an engineer testing variations.

None of them were dead. That was the thing. The ropes held them short of strangulation, the positions uncomfortable and terrifying, but not fatal. They hung above the deck and called out to one another and to the men below who were still free, and the freed ran to those bound and tried to unravel them but the ropes tightened when hands came near to assist and the freemen were lashed back.

The tar came next.

It seeped upward through the deck planking — not down, not through gaps and cracks the way tar worked when heat drew it, but upward, against gravity, finding the seams between planks and rising through them in slow black threads that spread across the deck surface and connected and spread further, covering the planking in a skin of black that was warm to the touch and smelled of something older than the ship, older than the tar itself, something that the tar was merely carrying much like water carries whatever has been dissolved in it.

Men who stepped in it found it slow to release their boots. Not impossible, not the suction of deep mud, but reluctantly, as a hand resists when it does not want to let go.

The bilge water came up through the pump housing. Not spilling but traveling, moving upward through the pipes with a pressure that had no physical source, spreading across the deck to join the tar, and where the two met they did not mix but simply occupied the same space with an easy coexistence of things that belong together.

And through it all, something invisible but a shape that could still be discerned moved among the suspended men and the tar-covered deck of men trying to reach their crew mates, something with red eyes and no explainable form moved with the unhurried pleasure of something surveying territory it has just seized.

The crew could track it by what happened around it. A man thrown six feet to port with nothing visible touching him. A lantern crushed in its housing, the glass imploding inward rather than outward, a flame extinguished by something that did not need hands to extinguish it. The rope holding Bertrand tightened by two inches precisely as the presence passed beneath him, Bertrand's grunt of compressed pain marked its passage like a buoy marks a current.

The stride in its step was unbothered...unhurried.

For it had nowhere it needed to be.

* * *

It moved below.

The crew saw it descend, or more precisely felt it descend, its departure made evident by the departure of a pressure that had been pressing on your chest and had briefly eased. The men, still free on deck, moved immediately to the suspended men, reaching for the ropes with knives, cutting what they could reach, bringing three of the five down in the first minute. Bertrand came down hard and lay on the tar-covered deck not moving, and the man who reached him first put a hand on his chest and felt breathing and called out that he was alive, and the relief in the call was the most human sound the deck had produced in an hour.

Below, in the passage outside Moreau's cabin, the sound changed.

The men nearest the passage entrance heard it first. A sound that the ship's timbers were not supposed to make, a low resonant pulse that was not mechanical nor structural, the sound of the wood itself doing something wood was not created to do. Some of them recognized it from the night the hold had been sealed. Some of them had not been on deck that night and were beholding it for the first time.

Those who recognized it moved away from the passage entrance.

Those who did not, moved toward it because a good crewman moved toward trouble, it was what you did; it was the training and the habit and the identity of a man who had chosen this work, and some of them would spend the rest of their lives understanding that their training had nearly killed them.

"Captain!" The call went toward Moreau's door. "Captain, get out! Get out now, it's coming..."

* * *

Moreau heard them.

He heard the specific fear in their voices. The fear of men who had seen something and were reporting it rather than imagining it, and he had spent thirty years learning to distinguish between those two categories and his discernment, was correct now.

He did not move from his position against the far wall.

He picked up both pistols and held one in each hand and aimed them at the door and waited, and in the waiting, he was entirely himself. Thirty years distilled to this, to the stillness and the level aim and the refusal to move from the position he had chosen, which was an inferior position by any tactical assessment and yet was the only position available—that of his back against a wall.

The door opened.

He fired.

The flash and the report in the enclosed cabin space were enormous, the sound hit the walls and echoed back, and the powder smoke filled the air immediately; through the smoke he could see the red eyes.

He fired again and heard — heard, did not see. The sound of a ball striking something that was not the red eyes, but something behind them.

A man. One of his crew. A crewman who had stood in the passage behind the presence, a damnable innocent in the wrong place at the wrong time, a man whose name Moreau knew and whose family he did not know, and the ball had gone through the space the red eyes occupied — through, not stopped, and had found the man behind them.

The crewman fell.

Moreau was already reloading. His hands moved through the loading sequence with the speed of long practice: powder and ball and ram; motions so deeply trained they did not require conscious attention.

He raised the reloaded pistol when the gun was removed from his hand.

He felt it go. Felt the grip on the pistol first, something closing around the barrel with a force that was not large but was completely precise, and then the pistol was out of his hand and in front of his face and the barrel was being bent.

The iron of the tube folded. Slowly. Deliberately. Not snapped — folded, with the patient application of force that had no visible source, the metal yielding against a force unseen. A bending of iron by the will and strength of an entity beyond the strength of men. The barrel bent at the middle until the two halves were at ninety degrees to each other, and then the bent pistol was lowered and placed on the chart table with a carefulness that was both terrifying and purposeful, sat down gently beside the spinning compass. A physical token that expressed that there was no force that would prevail against what presence was in the room with him.

Moreau looked at it.

Looked with the expression of a man revising his understanding of what the world contained.

Then he looked at the doorway and the men attempting to attend to the dead crewmen not far away.

And in that moment when he was not concerned for himself...he was taken by the left leg.

He felt the grip of a hand on his ankle, felt it through his boot, the pressure of something closing with the certainty of something that did not need to hurry because the outcome had already been determined. Within that split second he had one moment of complete understanding, the kind of clarity that arrives in the final seconds before impact, and in that moment he thought of his daughters, his compass, and the man he had shot through the thing that had nobody; and thought: I should have run.

Then he was moving, dragged like a dog's toy along the floor of his cabin.

The speed of it was the first shock. He moved across the cabin floor before his body could fully register the motion, the transition from standing, to horizontal, to moving happened in the space between one heartbeat and the next, and then he was through the doorway and in the passage, and the passage walls were on both sides of him and he was traveling fast through the narrow walls to this left and right.

His left arm hit the passage wall. The sound it made was the sound that bones make when they encounter something unyielding at speed, and the pain that followed was the kind of pain that clarifies everything, that strips the world down to the single fact of itself, and Moreau heard his own voice release a sound he had not made since he was a child.

His right leg hit the opposite wall. The angle was wrong for a leg to meet a wall at that speed, and his body registered the wrongness completely, immediately, and with agony.

He passed his men.

He saw them upside down, or at the wrong angle, the passage tilted by his position and his speed. He saw their faces as he passed them and noted within their faces the particular horror of men watching something happen to someone they cannot help, and he saw hands reaching for him and falling back because whatever held his ankle was not a thing that hands could interfere with, and he saw Renard, who had made it back from the hold attempt to intervene and then was violently pressed against the passage wall with both arms extended. His face open in a way Moreau had never seen it open in eleven years, and he wanted to tell Renard something, but time was not his ally, and the pain of broken bones masked words that could not come over his screams.

His right arm hit the ladder housing.

The passage opened into the hold anteroom and the hold door was ahead of him and open, and within the opening was the black of the hold. Moreau understood that he was going into that and from the dark into the eternal night and he ushered strength, courage, and fear and sought to stop his descent into what his mind viewed as the end of his existence.

He tried to grip the doorframe as he passed it. His hand found the wood and held for a fraction of a second and in that fraction of a second the thing holding his ankle pulled, and the arm held, and the physics of the situation resolved in the way that physics resolves when something has to give against an unyielding force.

And Moreau's arm was what gave. And it torn from his body at the shoulder.

Cleanly. With the efficiency of something that knew human anatomy and had applied that knowledge without waste.

The arm remained in the door frame, Moreau's hand still curved around the wood, fingers still holding the shape of the grip that had failed to hold him.

The hold door then closed behind him.

* * *

The screaming lasted forty seconds.

The men in the passage stood with the door between them and the hold, and their ears were assaulted for forty seconds of screams and the cracking of bone. Forty seconds none of them would ever lose or speak of in precise terms afterward, forty seconds that would wake them at three in the morning for the rest of their lives and place them back in the passage with the door between them and the dark and the sounds of a dying man that came through the wood.

Then there was silence.

The particular silence that Antoine had described to Lescaut before they descended. The silence of a room in which tasks have been completed.

They stood in the passage.

Renard looked at the arm in the doorframe. He looked at it for a long time. Then reached out and took it and cradled it against his chest and stood with it.

No one said anything.

Nobody moved.

The hold door then opened.

Antoine emerged.

He came up through the hold anteroom and into the passage, and he looked at the assembled men, each gawking in terror and awe. Renard with his burden, the others pressed against the walls, all those faces that had heard the forty seconds and his own face was the face it had been when he had come off the deck after the compass conversation with Moreau, the face that he had cultivated for weeks. A face that was composed. Present. Yet, slightly removed from the situation, in the way a man who is managing a complex enterprise encounters an unexpected logistical development.

He looked at Renard. Then he looked at what Renard was holding.

Something moved in his face: briefly, insufficiently, a shadow of his humanity that should have been there for all to see, but then was gone.

"It wants the trunk moved to my quarters," he said.

His voice was the voice of a man relaying an administrative declaration. Clear. Measured. A voice used for commission papers, cargo manifests, and ration disputes.

The men looked at him.

Renard looked at him over the thing he was holding against his chest, and his face was not the face of a man who was going to speak, not yet, not having experienced the events and seen the sights he had just seen, not with forty seconds of screams that still echoed in his ears. Not with the weight of bloody flesh, he held in his arms.

Antoine met his eyes and did not look away.

"The trunk," he said again. "To my quarters. Tonight."

He turned to move through the men and nobody moved to stop him.

He walked through the assembled men as water moves through a space — finding the path of least resistance, the bodies parting before him not out of respect, but out of something that had no name yet on this ship, something that would have a name by morning perhaps, something that looked at Antoine de la Mothe Cadillac and understood, without being able to articulate it, that the thing in the hold had not taken him, and for whatever the reason the creature had not taken him the exploration was not an effort any of them wanted to examine too closely.

He went up to the deck.

And unknown to all, the compass in his dead captain's cabin was still spinning.

While in the hold, patient as it had always been, the trunk waited to be moved.

Chapter Sixteen

The Rebellion

Nobody slept.

That was the first thing — the ship's night watch, which should have rotated in the orderly rhythm of a working vessel, simply did not. The men who should have gone below stayed above. The men who were below came up. The distinction between watch and off watch dissolved in the hours after the hold door closed, and what replaced it was something older and less organized: the instinct of a group of frightened people to be together, to have bodies near them, to not be alone in a dark space with the sounds of the ship around them.

Renard let this happen. He stood at the passage entrance with Moreau's arm wrapped in canvas in his arms and he watched his crew make their decision and he did not issue orders to countermand it, because the orders would not have been followed and issuing orders that would not be followed was worse than not issuing them. He had learned this from Moreau. He had learned most things from Moreau. He was aware of this in a way that was not grief yet — grief required more space than the current situation allowed — but was something adjacent to it, something that would become grief when there was time.

He sent two men to the hold door. Gros and a Flemish deckhand named Pieters, chosen because they were large and because they had not been in the passage when Moreau was taken and therefore had a marginally better relationship with their own composure than the men who had been. He told them to stand at the door and not to open it under any circumstances, and not to touch the door if it moved of its own accord, and to come find him immediately if anything changed.

Gros looked at him. "And if it comes through the door?"

"Run," Renard said.

He went back to the deck.

* * *

Antoine was at the starboard rail when Renard came up through the hatch. He was standing with his hands on the wood, face out toward the water, the posture of a man who has arranged himself to appear as though he is thinking about something other than what he is thinking about. The night was clear, the Atlantic enormous and indifferent around them, and the ship was moving in its slow possessed way, the rigging managing itself, the deck planking still tacky in places with the dark substance that was not tar or was tar that had been something else.

Several men were on deck. They were not gathered around Antoine: they were positioned at various points, doing nothing in particular, not looking at him directly, and the not-looking was its own kind of looking, the specific attention of men who are tracking a thing without appearing to track it.

Renard crossed the deck and stood beside Antoine at the rail, and for a moment they were simply two men at the rail in the dark.

"The arm," Antoine said. He did not look at Renard. "He should be given the full committal. When it's light enough."

"Yes," Renard said.

"The men who were suspended. Are they..."

"Three are ambulatory. Bertrand has broken ribs and cannot stand without assistance. The fifth..." Renard paused. "The fifth has not spoken since we brought him down. The surgeon..." he stopped. The surgeon was Lescaut. The surgeon was in the hold. "Thomas Mercer is seeing to him."

Antoine nodded. "Good."

"The hold door," Renard said. "I have men on it. We will not move the trunk until daylight."

"No," Antoine said. "We'll move it now."

Renard looked at him for the first time. "I have two men at that door who agreed to stand there because it was daylight they were waiting for. If I send them in there now..."

"The trunk will be moved now," Antoine said. His voice was not loud and not hard. It was the voice of a man stating a fact about the weather. "It asked for tonight. It won't wait for daylight."

Renard looked at him. His look was the look of a man who was adding information to a total that was becoming very large and very clear.

"I'll get four men," Renard said finally.

"Two is enough."

"I'll get four men," Renard said again. The same words. The same tone. The specific repetition of a man who has one piece of authority remaining and is exercising it.

Antoine returned to looking at the water. "As you like."

* * *

The trunk was moved at the second hour past midnight.

Four men went into the hold, each with a lantern. They moved quickly, and they did not look at the planking, and they did not look at each other and they lifted the trunk between two of them while the other two held the lanterns at maximum extension away from their bodies, as if the lanterns were themselves something to be cautious about. The trunk was heavier than it should have been and the men carrying it felt this and adjusted their grip and did not comment on it.

They brought it up the ladder and through the passage to Antoine's berth without incident. They set it against the wall where he indicated. He thanked them. They left.

In the passage outside his berth, one of them was sick against the wall.

Another one, a young sailor named Coste who had been at sea for two years and who had joined this expedition because the land grant had seemed worth the risk, sat down on the passage floor and put his face in his hands and stayed there for some time. No one told him to move. When he finally stood and went back to the deck, nobody asked him about it.

* * *

The hour before dawn was the quietest hour.

Not peaceful, but quiet in the way that the twenty seconds before a storm arrives are quiet. The particular silence of everything drawing breath simultaneously. The men on deck moved very little. The men below moved very little. The ship itself moved with its new unnatural ease, finding its heading without a hand on the wheel, the rigging adjusted by nothing visible, and if you did not look at the wheel turning on its own or the lines moving without hands on them you could almost pretend, in the dark and the quiet, that you were on an ordinary ship making an ordinary crossing.

Almost.

Renard stood by the mainmast and looked at the wheel, turning and did not pretend.

He was thinking about the institution. He had been thinking about it since he wrapped Moreau's arm in canvas — the institution of the ship, the chain of command, the regulations and customs and accumulated practical wisdom of men who had worked out over centuries how to keep a floating wooden box pointed in the right direction with enough men alive to sail it. He was the first mate. The first mate's function was defined by the captain's existence. He existed to support the captain, to extend the captain's authority, to be the mechanism through which the captain's decisions became the ship's reality.

The captain was in the hold.

Renard was now the captain. This was the regulation, this was what happened: the first mate assumed command. He had assumed command of three ships in his career under varying circumstances and had done it each time with the automatic facility of a man who had trained for exactly this and was ready.

He had not trained for this.

He looked at the wheel and thought about what assuming command actually meant on this ship, tonight, with the wheel turning on its own and four men suspended in the rigging two hours ago and a thing in the hold that had bent iron in front of a man's eyes and then dragged that man through his own passage by the leg.

He thought about Antoine at the rail. The voice that stated facts about weather. Two is enough.

He thought about Moreau's arm in canvas.

He thought about what assuming command meant when the thing that was actually commanding the ship did not have a rank he could address.

* * *

Antoine came out of his berth at first light.

He was dressed. His coat was on and his documents were under his arm and his face was the face that it had been since the passage. The face of a man managing a complex enterprise. He came through the hatch onto the deck and stood in the early light and looked at the assembled crew with the assessing eye of a man taking stock of his resources.

There were thirty-one men left. He counted them. Thirty-one, plus the passengers sealed below, plus the possessed men who occupied a category he did not include in his operational accounting because their usefulness was no longer his to direct.

He opened his mouth to speak.

Gros hit him with the belaying pin.

***

It was not a glancing blow. Gros had spent the night at the hold door and what he had spent it thinking about had resolved into something simple and direct, and he swung the belaying pin with the full weight of a large man's arm and his grief and his fear and his thirty years of knowing Moreau, and Antoine went down.

He went down hard and did not immediately get up.

For a moment — two seconds, perhaps three — nobody moved. The deck held its breath.

Then the men moved.

Not all of them. Not even most of them. But enough: eight men, ten, moving from different positions on the deck toward where Antoine had fallen, and what they carried was what they had at hand, which was belaying pins and a knife and in one case bare hands, and their faces had the particular expression of men who have decided that calculation is over and action is what remains. They had watched their captain taken apart. They had listened to forty seconds; they would never lose. They had stood in the passage and watched a man pass through it on his way to something they would not name and had been unable to do anything, and here was something they could do, something that could be reached and struck, something that was lying on the deck in front of them not moving.

Renard put himself between them and Antoine.

He did not draw a weapon. He did not shout. He stood in front of the prone figure of Antoine de la Mothe Cadillac with his hands at his sides and his body in the path of the men coming, and he said:

"No."

One word. The voice of a man who has been the first mate for eleven years and understands that the first mate's function is to be the last institutional structure standing when everything else has failed, and has decided that the institution will stand here, in this moment, even if he cannot articulate a rational argument for why it should.

Gros stopped. The others stopped behind him.

"He's the reason..." Gros started.

"Yes," Renard said.

"Moreau is..."

"Yes."

"Then why are you..."

"Because killing him doesn't change what's in the hold," Renard said. "And killing him might make it worse. And I don't know what it will do if we touch him and I am not prepared to find out without knowing." He looked at Gros. He looked at the men behind Gros. He looked at them the way Moreau had looked at mutinous men, without flinching, without the performance of calm, with the actual thing, which was not the absence of fear but the presence of something that had decided the fear was not the relevant consideration. "We need to reach Quebec. That is the only thing that matters. We need to reach Quebec with enough men alive to sail the ship. Everything else is secondary."

"He's not secondary," Gros said. His voice had cracked on the last word. He had been at the hold door for hours with the sounds of Moreau in his ears, and the crack was the sound of something that had been held tightly for a long time releasing the pressure of its holding.

"No," Renard said. "He's not." He held Gros's eyes. "But killing him here, on this deck, with that thing in the hold watching: that's not justice. That's theater. And I'm not going to let you perform for it."

The silence stretched.

Antoine moved. He was pushing himself upright, one hand on the deck, the motion of a man whose body is reporting damage and who is attending to the report and continuing, anyway. He got to his knees. He got to his feet. He stood.

The side of his face was dark where the belaying pin had found it. He touched the place with two fingers: clinical, assessing, and looked at the blood on his fingers, and looked at Gros, and looked at Renard.

He said nothing.

He picked up his documents from where they had fallen and straightened them, and put them back under his arm.

Renard watched him do this. Something moved through Renard's face; not in his expression, which remained what it had been, but behind his expression, in the place where a man's actual relationship with what he is seeing lives.

"Get below," Renard said. To Antoine. Quietly. "Stay in your berth until I come for you."

Antoine looked at him. For a moment, but just a moment as something in his face shifted, something that might have been the thing that should have been there all along, the thing that had been briefly present in the hold when Lescaut had looked at him over his folded stole and said you're not sorry. It was there for the duration of a breath and then it was gone, and his face was the face it had been.

He went below.

The men watched him go.

Gros was still holding the belaying pin. He looked at it as if he had forgotten it was in his hand, and then he put it down on the deck and sat down beside it and put his face in his hands and made a sound that was not crying and was not anything else that had a name.

Renard looked at the wheel. Turning. Steady. Pointing them where it intended to point them.

He thought: We need to reach Quebec.

He thought: And then what?

He had no answer for the second thought, so he stayed with the first one and let it be enough.

***

The dispersal took twenty minutes.

Men drifted to their posts or to the positions that had become their posts in the new arrangement — the deck, the rail, the hatch, the places where being in proximity to other men felt marginally safer than the alternative. The crisis had peaked and broken, and what remained was the exhaustion that followed crisis, the flat gray aftermath where the body has used what it had and has not yet begun to replenish it.

Renard remained by the mainmast. He watched the men settle. He watched Bertrand, helped by two others, make his painful way to the rail and grip it and stand looking at the water the way a man stands at a rail when he needs the horizon to be real. He watched Coste sit against the foremast with his knees up and his head back, and his eyes closed, not sleeping — nobody was sleeping — just resting with his eyes closed in the morning light.

He watched the hold door. Gros and Pieters had resumed their posts there, or Gros had, Pieters was somewhere on the deck, Renard would find him in a minute. Gros sat against the door with the belaying pin across his knees and his face pointed forward and his eyes showing the specific quality of a man who is not going to sleep and is not going to move and has decided that these are the two things he can control and is controlling them.

The ship was quiet.

The wheel turned.

Renard thought: Twenty minutes. I have had twenty minutes of quiet.

He knew, the way a man who has been at sea for thirty years knows weather, that twenty minutes was what he was going to get.

* * *

They heard it before they understood it.

A sound from the hold anteroom: not from the hold itself, not through the door that Gros was sitting against: from the passage that ran alongside the hold, the secondary access that was used for cargo inspection and had not been used for anything since Moreau's arm had been left in the doorframe of the primary entrance. A sound that was not quite a voice and was not quite anything else, something that occupied the frequency between sounds, the register that the ear caught without being able to fully resolve into language.

But two men resolved it into language.

Two men who had been standing near the secondary passage entrance, who had been assigned there by Renard to watch it, who had been standing there in the gray morning light with their backs to the hold and their faces to the deck and who had been, until approximately ninety seconds ago, as reliably themselves as any men on the ship.

Renard saw them change.

It was not dramatic. It was the opposite of dramatic; it was a settling, a relaxation, the tension going out of their posture like tension releases from a rope when the load it is bearing is removed. Their shoulders dropped. Their heads tilted at an angle that was not quite the angle a head tilts when a man is listening to something he is trying to understand, but the angle a head tilts when a man is listening to something he already understands completely and is simply receiving.

They looked at each other.

Then they looked at the deck.

***

The first one moved before Renard could reach him.

His name was Fortier, a Norman sailor, forty-three years old, eleven years on Atlantic crossings, a man who had stood at the hold door two nights ago and had been one of the three who had gone to Renard and asked to be posted anywhere else. He moved with the fluid absence of hesitation that Antoine had and Moreau had never had, the movement of something that had offloaded the weight of deliberation. He crossed the deck in eight steps, and the knife was in his hand, and he took Coste, sitting against the foremast with his eyes closed in the morning light, not sleeping, just resting. He took Coste across the throat with the efficiency of something that had decided on the outcome before it began moving and was merely executing the decision.

Coste did not make a sound.

The second man, Lemaire, younger, a carpenter's mate, moved in the opposite direction toward the group of men at the port rail. He did not have a knife. He had his hands, and what he did with his hands in the next four seconds showed that whatever was directing him had a thorough working knowledge of what hands could accomplish when the man they belonged to had been freed from his own reluctance to use them.

Two men went into the water. One of them could not swim. The Atlantic received them both with identical indifference.

The deck erupted.

* * *

The chaos that followed was of the specific type that is worst to be inside — not the chaos of a storm or a fire, which has a logic and a direction and an enemy that can be identified and addressed, but the chaos of a community turning on itself, where the threat is wearing the faces of people you know and the threat does not know it is a threat and is not distinguishable from the man next to you until it is too late to distinguish.

Fortier had been at sea for eleven years. Men had sailed with him. Men had eaten beside him and complained about the rations beside him and held him steady when the storms came. His face was his face. His hands were his hands. The knife was new.

Three men dead in four minutes.

The fourth minute was the one where the loyal crew understood what they were dealing with and the understanding did not help because knowing a thing and being able to address it were not the same thing, and the possessed men moved without the hesitation that knowing produced, and the loyal men moved with it, and the difference was four minutes and three men and the specific expression on Renard's face as he tried to reach Fortier and could not get there in time.

He got there in time for the fifth man.

He hit Fortier from behind, not a careful blow, not a measured application of force, but the full-weight impact of a large man who had run across a deck and thrown himself at another large man. They went down together, and Renard got the knife hand and held it against the deck and looked into Fortier's face.

Fortier looked back at him.

His face was Fortier's face. That was the thing: Renard had expected something else, some visible difference, some sign of what had replaced the man he knew. But the face was his face. The eyes were his eyes, brown and ordinary, the same color they had always been. Whatever the thing in the hold had put in him did not change his face.

"Fortier," Renard said.

Fortier looked at him with his own eyes and said nothing.

"Fortier!" Louder. The way you speak to a man who has been knocked and is coming back.

Nothing.

Renard hit him. Hard, across the jaw, with the side of his fist. Fortier's head snapped sideways and when it came back, his eyes were closed. Renard took the knife and stood up and looked at the deck.

Lemaire was on the deck three yards away, held by two men, not struggling. His face had the same quality as Fortier's — present, his own, evacuated of whatever had been directing it. The thing that had whispered to him had used him and moved on.

The deck was silent.

Four men were down. Three of them were not getting up. The fourth was Coste against the foremast, and he was not getting up either, and the morning light fell on him with the same quality it had fallen on him when he had been sitting there with his eyes closed resting, and the light did not know the difference, and the ship did not know the difference, and the Atlantic certainly did not know the difference.

Renard stood in the middle of the deck and looked at what four minutes had produced.

He heard, faintly, from somewhere, from the hold, from the rigging, from the grain of the wood or the frequency between sounds, something that was not quite laughter.

He had heard it before.

He recognized it.

He did not look for its source because he already knew what he would find if he found it, and he had enough in his hands already.

He looked at his crew. At what remained of his crew. Thirty-one had become twenty-four in the last four minutes. Twenty-four men to sail a ship that did not need sailing, to guard a hold that could not be guarded, to protect passengers sealed below decks from a thing that had already demonstrated that protection was a concept it found mildly entertaining.

He thought: Quebec.

He thought: We need to reach Quebec.

He thought: God help the people at Quebec when we do.

He had no answers for any of these thoughts so he put them aside and started organizing what was left, because that was what the first mate did, and if he was going to be any use to anyone for the rest of this crossing, he was going to do what he had trained to do and he was going to keep doing it until he couldn't.

Moreau had taught him that, too.

He started with the dead. You started with the dead because you owed them that and because the living needed to see you start there. You did not leave your people on the deck.

You began with the names.

He began with the names.

Chapter Seventeen

The Ship Breathes

It began with the bell.

The ship's bell, mounted at the foremast, rang once at the third hour past midnight with no hand near it and no wind to move it — a single clear tone that crossed the deck and fell into the water and was gone. The men who heard it looked at the bell and looked at each other and did not speak. They had developed, in the last hours, a collective economy of speech that reserved words for things that required them and let everything else pass in silence. The bell did not require words. The bell was simply the bell, ringing on its own, which was one more thing on a ship that had been full of such things for days, and the men looked at it and looked away and waited for whatever came next.

And what came next was the silence.

It did not creep in. It did not arrive gradually, the way silence arrives at the end of a conversation when the last speaker finishes and the quiet expands to fill the void words had occupied. It arrived all at once, total and immediate, the way a door closes. The sound of the Atlantic against the hull, the creak of the rigging, the small percussive language of a working ship, the breathing of the men, all of it present one moment and then absent the next, replaced by something that was not the absence of sound but was itself a presence, thick, weighted and oppressive. In the same manner, a chest is compressed by the weight of iron upon one's sternum.

Renard heard his own heartbeat.

He heard it because it affirmed he remained in the land of the living and because the silence had the quality of a space specifically arranged to make that single sound audible. He put his hand on his chest. Felt its beat. It was steady. He was grateful for this in a way that was wholly new to him: the gratitude of a man who had discovered that his body continued to function without being asked, and he found this remarkable.

Around him, the men were still.

Not frozen, still. A stillness akin to the quiet of nature before the unleashing of a gale. They had their weapons; the belaying pins, the knives, the two pistols that Renard had redistributed after the chaos, and their hands were on their weapons and thought they knew none of that mattered the hands stayed where they were because hands needed a place to be. Hands that clutched the triggers and handles as Catholics hold to their rosaries.

The wind died.

Not diminished — died. One moment the Atlantic wind did as winds do, moving through the rigging with its constant low voice, pressing against the canvas with its insistent directional weight, and the next moment it did not. The canvas went slack. The rigging, which had been managing itself in the ship's newly possessed way, simply stopped moving and hung where it was, motionless, as if the air itself had decided to stop participating.

The ship slowed.

The momentum of the crossing carrying it forward through water that was suddenly still, the swells flattened in a radius around the vessel as if the water were making room. The ocean drew back from the ship as people who draw back from a person with leprosy. Seagulls squawked to the sharks below as if to told nature, *"unclean."*

The ship drifted through the stillness of its own making.

And then the deck moved.

Not the movement of a ship in water: not the pitch nor yaw of the slow Atlantic roll that had been the texture of every moment since La Rochelle. An unnatural movement. A movement from within the bowels of the vessel itself.

The deck planks swelled.

It was subtle to the eye—but noticeable. Swelling similar to the slight puffs of escaping water within a teapot before one hears the banshee-like scream of water boiling. The planks swelled along their length; wood expanded in the way that wood expands when it absorbs moisture from long exposure. The seams between planks closed slightly, and the surface rose by a fraction of an inch across the entire deck simultaneously.

It was wrong. The air was dry. The air had been dry for days. There was nothing to expand the wood. And yet the wood did not care about the laws of nature.

Renard crouched and put his palm flat on the deck. He felt it against his palm. The warmth of the wood had changed. A solid things carved by the cunning of man's hands and pressed into service to bear him across the sea no longer felt like wood, but radiated the warmth of a living thing rather than timber, and under the heat a vibration that was too slow and too regular to be structural, too intentional to be mechanical. Too alive.

He straightened up and looked at his hand.

Then the wood pulsed.

Once.

A single contraction and release, moving through the deck planking like a wave moving through water, traveling from the stern forward and passing under the men's feet and continuing to the bow and subsiding. The men felt it in their boots and in their legs, and in their teeth. Several of them made sounds. And none were the sounds of words.

Silence.

Then twice.

The second pulse came from below: from somewhere deep within the hull itself, from the ribs, keel, and the deep structural timber that held the ship's shape. A pulse that traveled upward through the planking, and did not subside but continued, slower, and sustained, a rhythm establishing itself in the bones of the vessel like a newborn heartbeat establishes itself and announces with a wail that a child has entered the earth.

The ship was breathing.

Not the mechanical rhythm of pumps or the structural flex of timber under load. A rhythm: slow, deep, and regular, the rhythm of something very large drawing breath, and like the ancient Kraken of lore, Renard swore to the God of Heaven that his ship, the La Vigilante, now lived.

The wood pulsed again. And again. Settling into its rhythm. Finding it. The deck under their feet, the hull around them, the masts above them, all of it breathing together, one organism, one breath, in and out, in and out. The sound of timber splintering and expanding assaulted the ears.

Renard stood in the middle of the deck and felt the ship breathe under him and thought, with the calm clarity of a man whose mind has gone past the uncharted territory of fear, realized it was not the men. It has never been the men.

The men.

Multiple possessed men. Fortier with his own face and empty eyes. Lemaire with his hands. The ones who had knelt in the rigging and the ones who had whispered to each other in the dark and the ones who had been managed and directed and used. He had been thinking about the men. He had been concerned about their possible possession, concerned about individual people inciting mutiny. He entertained fears about the creature using his crew against one another. He had been thinking about it as a personnel problem, as a problem of identifying, containing, and managing compromised individuals. Thinking like a doctor might manage a virus.

He realized now, too late, that how he saw the problem was the problem.

The men were not the concern for possession. The men were the symptoms of possession. The ship was the thing possessed. The ship had always been the house for this demonic tenant, from the moment the trunk came aboard at La Rochelle, since the first night the banging started, since the compass sat wrong in two men's pockets simultaneously. The creature had not moved into the crew. The creature had moved into the vessel, and the crew had been the vessel's instruments, human hands the ship's appendages, the way a ship's rigging is the ship's instrument.

The Nain Rouge had not taken his men.

It had taken a ship.

***

The possessed men knelt.

Not all at once — sequentially, one after another, beginning at the stern and proceeding forward, each man going to his knees as the pulse passed through the deck beneath him, as if the deck were invoking a call to worship and the men responded in-kind. The kneeling, the ancient response to something felt through the soles of the boots that the loyal men could feel too but did not respond to in the same way because whatever this call to worship was, it was an evil clarion not open to them. Renard concluded whatever hold the creature held over the possessed was a compulsion tuned to a voice only they could hear.

They knelt how you kneel when you are recognizing something you worship. Not submission, but recognition. Similar to how a dog lies down when its owner enters the room without being told, out of the simple animal knowledge of who is in the room and what that means.

Seven men. Eight. The ones the creature had been working with since early in the crossing, the ones Renard had been watching, the ones who had moved without hesitation and looked at him with familiar faces and empty eyes. They knelt on the breathing deck and put their hands flat on the planking and bowed their heads and the ship breathed around them and through them and they were very still.

The loyal men looked at the kneeling men and then at each other and then at Renard.

Renard had nothing to give them. He had his presence and his function and the long habit of a man who kept doing his work, and he gave them what he had, which was standing in the middle of the deck without flinching, and it was not enough, and it was what there was. Somewhere within him, he remembered words he had read somewhere. Word that stayed with him. Perhaps as a boy, words he perhaps heard from his loving mother. Words he now voiced.

"Lord, remember us."

* * *

The first plank opened at the stern.

It did not break. It did not split, or crack, or warp, or do any of the things that planks do when they fail, when wood gives under stress or rots under the slow, methodical work of water and time. It simply parted, the seam between two planks widening with the precise deliberateness of lips parting, not forced, not strained, just opening. Wood on each side of the seam stayed intact and sound and functioning as wood, yet simply no longer touched the wood beside it.

The opening was six inches wide and ran the width of a plank, three feet of darkness, and the darkness below it was not the darkness of the bilge or the hold or any space that had a name and a purpose. It was the darkness of an interior that had become like an abyss, a hollowed void of encroaching ebony. The darkness of the ship's new self.

The man standing nearest to it looked down.

His name was Auber. He was twenty-eight. He had a wife in Normandy and two daughters whose names he said to himself every morning upon waking, a ritual he had developed on long crossings to keep the fact of them real and close. He had not been among the possessed. He had been among the most reliably himself of any man on the ship — cautious and observant and not given to the panic that had taken others, managing his fear with the focused practicality of a man who had decided that fear was information and information was useful and panic was neither. Renard considered a good man...devout even.

He looked down into the opening.

He was close to it, two feet, perhaps less, and what he saw in it made him step back, and the step back took him over the plank behind him, and he went down on one knee and in the moment of his imbalance the deck changed.

The plank opened further. Not toward him, not reaching, not grasping, nothing so directed as that. It simply opened more, the seam widening to a foot, the darkness deepening, and Auber's knee was on the planking beside it and then his knee was at the edge of it and then his knee was over it and then he was in it.

He went the way water descends into a drain, not pulled, not dragged, simply drawn by the pull of gravity, and the opening was just wide enough and no wider, and it closed behind him with the same deliberateness with which it had opened, the planks returning to their positions, fitting back against each other with the neat precision of joinery, the seam closing to nothing.

The deck was solid where he had been.

For three seconds, perhaps four, nothing remained of Auber on the surface of the deck. The loyal crew stood and looked at the place and the place showed them nothing.

Then the wood moved.

The grain of the planking at the place where the seam had been shifted slightly, the lines of the wood rearranging themselves in a way that wood did not rearrange, and what emerged from the rearrangement was a face.

Not clearly. Not as a carving or an impression or anything that could be attributed to the natural pattern of grain and knot. A face I the manner that a face emerges from a cloud, or how a face emerges from any sufficiently complex visual field when the eye is primed to look for one — but more than that, more than pareidolia, because the eye did not need to be primed and the features did not need to be sought. They were simply there. Present. Looking up from the wood with the expression of a man who has just understood something enormous and could no longer speak to convey it.

Auber's eyes. Open. Looking up through the wood at the deck and the sky and the men who were looking down at him with the expressions they would carry for the rest of their lives.

His mouth was open.

He had a mouth that did not scream.

And the living could not hear him.

***

The deck opened again. And again.

Not in sequence, not in the orderly progression of a thing working its way down a list, but in the way where multiple things simultaneously were being addressed, without hierarchy, without preference.

Three openings. Four. Different sizes, different locations, each one finding a man who was near it, not the nearest man, not the most convenient man. Each man selected as a domestic cook lifts from a cupboard the correct ingredients to be mixed into a casserole.

The men moved the moment the second plank opened: moving away from the openings, toward each other, toward the masts which were solid and vertical and connected to the ship in a way that felt different from the deck, the masts being structural in a way the deck was not, or feeling that way, which was probably not true but was the distinction the mind made when it needed somewhere to stand that was not opening.

The ship accommodated each man's movement as the openings stalked them as a hunter eyes prey.

Not quickly. Not frantically, but with the patience of knowing that the outcome was never in question and is engaged with the process for its own sake.

Girard went next. Then a man whose name Renard did not know: a passenger's servant, traveling in the servant's capacity, a young man from Brittany who had been at sea for the first time and had spent the crossing in a state of comprehensive misery that had, in the last hours, been transmuted into something that was not quite acceptance but close to it. He went flailing into the deck between two planks that parted for him specifically, and when the planks closed and the grain shifted, what remained of his exposed face looked up.

However, his expression was different from Auber's. An expression of someone young encountering something so far outside the realm of their experience that the face had not been given the tools from the mind to respond to it and is simply present, in a terrified awe mingled with fear and the horror that one been unexpectedly chosen to meet their God or the blackness of the void. Each, no matter one's belief, a terrifying last thought to ponder.

And the faces in the wood accumulated.

Each looked up from the deck with various expressions: shock, confusion, the beginning of an understanding that would not be completed, something that in one or two of them looked almost like wonder, the wonder of a man who had encountered something so far beyond the scale of the ordinary world that the ordinary responses have been bypassed entirely and what remained was the pure fact of encountering the enormous. Most of them had their mouths and eyes wide open. Their terrified faces petrified in the wood of the La Vigilante.

None of them blinked.

And the wood did not obscure them; these faces were in the wood. No, the grain of the timber flowed around each face the way water flowed around stones. La Vigilante just incorporated the faces into her material, the wood now the medium through which the faces were expressed in the manner paint is the medium through which a portrait is revealed. You could see the grain of the timber through them. You could see the knots and the lines of the wood's history through them. And you could see them through the wood, looking up, present, unmistakably themselves.

And somehow, unmistakably... alive.

That was the worst thing.

Not that the faces were there — not that the ship had taken men and made them part of itself — but that the faces were still the faces of men who were alive in there, still present, still aware, still looking up through the planking at a deck and a sky they could no longer reach. Still registering. Still experiencing. Their groans and moans now carried aloft by the winds of the Atlantic.

Whatever the ship was doing to them, it had not ended them. No, it had incorporated them within itself, like a tree incorporates wire or stone into its growth, growing around and through what it encounters, making it part of itself, the wire or the stone becoming part of the tree without the tree or the wire being destroyed.

The men were in the ship.

They were part of the ship now.

And the ship was breathing.

***

Below decks, the passengers knew.

But what they did not know precisely, for they did not possess the vocabulary for what was happening above them, and they could not see through the planking nor open the hatches because the hatches had been sealed. Not locked, the mechanism of the latches was not engaged. The wood was simply holding the hatches closed like a man holds a door closed, with the simple continuous pressure that has decided the door will remain shut, neither concerned in the person's strength on the other side.

Blanchard had been the first to try the hatch first, because Blanchard was the man who tried things formally and documented the attempt. He put his shoulder to the hatch with the full weight of a large man behind it and yet the hatch did not move, again he tried, and it still did not move, and he stood back and looked at it and wrote something in the small notebook he had been keeping since La

Rochelle, because Blanchard was a notary and a notary recorded what he observed.

What he wrote was: The hatch does not open. The wood is warm.

He looked at what he had written, then added: The wood appears to be breathing.

He closed the notebook.

Sister Marie-Claire had already begun the Litany of the Saints. She had begun it quietly, almost under her breath, and then more strongly, and slowly other passengers joined her — not because they were instructed to, nor because they were following a leader, but because the litany was there and the litany was something to put in their mouths other than the sounds they wanted to make, and in the absence of any other tool the litany was the tool available, and Sister Marie-Claire's voice leading it was steady, and steady was what they needed.

"Sancta Maria, ora pro nobis.

Sancte Michael, ora pro nobis.

Sancte Joannes Baptista, ora pro nobis."

The responses came back in the various French and Flemish and one uncertain Latin of the assembled passengers, and the voices joined and the joining provided warmth in the sealed space, a luxury that the ship's new self had not yet touched or claimed or incorporated into its breathing.

Simone Aubert did not know yet that her husband was in the deck above her. She was holding her sons against her, one on each side, and saying the responses to the litany in a voice that her sons could hear and that was not shaking, because she was their mother and their mother's voice was a comfort and she would shelter them from the corporate fear they all felt for as long as it was in her power to keep it.

The younger boy said: "Where's Papa?"

"He's working," Simone said.

The boy accepted this because his mother's voice was steady and because he was nine and had not yet developed the machinery to doubt the things a mother says in that reassuring tone of voice.

She held him closer. Repeating to herself those words as if they were a confession to God.

The floor under her feet became warm.

She felt it through her shoes and looked down at the planking and she did not look at it for long because there was something akin to a man's face traveling through the grain of the wood and she had determined that she was not going to gaze at it further, that she was going to protect her sons from seeing the horrors of the adults fear for as long as she could maintain that protection.

She forced herself to look away and turned to look at Sister Marie-Claire, whose voice was leading the litany with the focused authority of a woman who had decided that this is what she would do in this moment. So the sister spoke her litany and gave herself to the task completely, not performing it, nor as a distraction, but to the actual doing of it, believing that the words were going somewhere and that the somewhere mattered and that the matter of it was worth her complete undivided attention.

Simone watched her and found something that was not quite comfort but was adjacent to it: the comfort of watching someone else be certain, which is not the same as being certain yourself but was better than nothing.

She said the response.

Above her...above them all, the deck breathed.

***

Commandant Antoine de la Mothe Cadillac stood at the mainmast.

He had come up when the first plank opened. He had heard something through the hull of his berth, a sound that was not the ship's ordinary voice, and had come up through the hatch before it sealed.

He stood at the main mast and watched.

He watched the planks open and close. Watched the faces emerge in the wood like flotsam. He watched Renard move among his men, his former men. The men who had been Moreau's men: trying to hold together what could be held together, trying to keep the remaining loyal crew from the openings, moving them back, keeping them at the masts and the rail and the structures that were not doing what the deck was doing, and found that the ship accommodated this, that the deck opened at the masts' bases but not directly at the masts themselves, as if there were a boundary there, as if the boundary were another piece of the creature's deliberateness.

The creature was not taking everyone.

Antoine had understood this from the first opening; from the way Auber had gone in and the men on either side of him had not. It was selective. It was choosing. It was working through the available material with the focused attention of something that knew what it wanted and took what it wanted and left behind the rest as refuse.

The men who had been loyal and functional were being taken. The possessed men, kneeling on the deck, were not being touched. The masts and the wheel, and the navigational instruments were intact. The ship's ability to move, to be steered, to function as a vessel: all intact, all operating. The rigging managing itself with its new possessed efficiency, the heading maintained, the speed steady.

The ship was not destroying itself.

The ship was culling itself.

Discarding what it no longer needed and incorporating the rest, leaving only what was required to complete the crossing.

Antoine watched Renard pull a man back from an opening and felt, briefly, insufficiently, the same shadow of the thing that had been there for a moment in the hold with Lescaut's stole folded in his hands. A feeling that was a ghost of what should have been there. It moved through him like an apparition and was gone before he could name it, and what remained was the familiar composed face and body standing at the mainmast in the early morning while the ship worked through its list.

He looked at his boots.

The deck was still firm under them.

It had been still under his boots since he came up through the hatch. It had not opened near him. It had not pulsed under his feet how it pulsed under the feet of the men being taken. The wood under him was warm and steady and present and entirely, utterly still, the eye of the storm, the one place on the deck that was not participating in what the rest of the deck was engaged in.

He understood why.

He had understood since the hold.

He was not a target. He was a passenger. His was the purpose of the crossing, the reason for the crossing, the thing that the crossing was in service of, and you did not absorb the purpose of the crossing into the deck planking, you delivered it.

He was cargo. A demonic means to an end.

He had made himself cargo when he drove the nail through Lescaut's palm. He had transferred himself from person to object, from the category of things that could be used to the category of things being transported, and the ship, the creature: knew the difference and was honoring it with the precise logic of something that had made a deal and was executing the deal's terms.

Antoine stood in the stillness of the deck that would not take him and watched the ship take his world apart plank by plank and face by face and kept his expression: his posture and held his documents under his arm.

He thought about the city he would found.

He always thought about the city.

* * *

Marguerite had come up through the hatch after him.

She had been below and Antoine had not seen her come up, nor heard the patter of the steps, she was simply there, the way she was always simply there, standing beside him at the mainmast in her traveling cloak with her dark hair braided back and her face wearing its expression, the one that had been waiting since La Rochelle.

She looked at the deck. At the faces in the wood. She looked at them with an expression that was not the expression of a child seeing something horrifying: it was the expression of a child seeing something she had been told about and is now observing the accuracy of the description.

She looked up at Antoine.

He looked down at her.

She put her hand in his.

Her hand was small and warm and entirely real, the hand of an eight-year-old girl, and it held his with the firm unconscious grip of a child who takes hold of an adult's hand when the adult needs it more than the child does.

He let her hold it. Took a mild comfort in her touch.

He looked out at the deck, at Renard and the remaining men gathered at the rail and the mast and the places that were not opening, at the kneeling possessed men with their hands flat on the breathing wood, at the faces looking up through the planking with their various expressions of the enormous, and he stood at the mainmast with a small hand in his and the city in his mind and the Atlantic around him in every direction, and the ship breathed under his feet, and the breathing was steady.

And the crossing of the Le Vigilante continued.

***

Renard counted.

He counted because counting was one for the few remaining things in his agency — the last tool available, the last form of order, the last thing that the situation had not taken from him. He counted the men still standing, still functional, still his in the sense that they were standing where he could see them and doing what he asked them to do.

Fourteen.

From thirty-one he had come to fourteen in the space of a night and a morning, and the night was not over, and the morning was not over, and the deck was still breathing, and the count was not final.

He looked at Antoine at the main mast. At the small hand in his. At the composed face looking out over the deck.

He looked at the faces in the wood.

He recognized some of them. He would not have been able to say which ones without looking more carefully than he was prepared to look, but he recognized some of them, much like you recognize people through a through a glass darkly, through something that interposes itself between you and the face and changes the quality of the recognition without eliminating it.

He recognized Auber's face in the deck. He did not know Auber's daughters' names. Had never known them, and would in all likelihood never know them, but he knew Auber spoke of them each morning, had heard him say their names in the berth, had never asked because a man's ritual was his own, and now the man was in the deck and the names were still in Renard's ear, twice a day, every morning, the way things stay in the ear.

He looked away from the deck.

He looked out at the horizon.

Somewhere in that direction was Quebec. He did not know how far. He had not been able to check the charts in the time that had been available to him for chart-checking, which was no time, which was the time a man had when his ship was doing what this ship was doing and there were fourteen men left and the deck has a face.

He looked at the wheel, turning on its own, holding the heading.

It knows where it's going. It has always known where it's going.

His thoughts continued: *Quebec is not where this ends. Quebec is where this thing arrives.*

He kept his eyes on the horizon and kept his count and kept his function and the ship breathed under his feet and the faces looked up from the deck and the morning light fell on all of it without distinction; the light doing what light did, illuminating without caring what it illuminated, which had always been the most honest thing about it.

Fourteen men.

The ship breathed.

The crossing continued.

Chapter Eighteen

The Crossing of the Remaining Days

The ship found its rhythm.

This was the thing that none of them had anticipated — not Renard, not Antoine, not the fourteen men who remained functional and who had organized themselves in the days after the deck breathed into something that was not quite a crew and was not quite a congregation and was not quite a group of survivors but contained elements of all three. All had expected continued horror. Each expected escalation and braced for the next thing, and the next thing, and the thing after that.

What they got instead was the ship moving.

Steadily. Purposefully and with the confidence of something that knows that nothing between here and there presented any obstacle worth the word to prevent it. The rigging managed itself. The heading held. The Atlantic was enormous and indifferent and occasionally violent — was simply the Atlantic, the swells reasonable, and the wind used by the ship with an efficiency that no human crew had achieved because no human crew had the complete attention of what was now managing the vessel.

The ship sailed beautifully.

This was the cruelest thing. After everything — after the compass and the trunk and the four men arranged like timber and the hold door and the captain's forty seconds and the deck that breathed and the faces in the planking — after all of it, the ship sailed beautifully, smooth and true and utterly indifferent to what it contained, and the days passed with the ordinary quality of days on an Atlantic crossing, light, dark and light again, the sun moving through its arc; the stars traveling their nightly circuit.

Renard stood at the helm that no longer needed him and kept his watch because keeping his watch was what he did and he had decided, in the days after the deck stopped breathing, that the doing of things was the last available form of dignity and he intended to maintain it.

The fourteen men organized themselves without being organized.

It happened in a way necessary things happened among practical people who had no authority structure left and no framework for establishing one: gradually, pragmatically, each man found what he could do, and the others accommodated the doing until a pattern emerged that was not a plan but functioned like one.

Gros took the food. He had always been the man most invested in the rations; the crossing's informal accountant of provisions, the man who knew to the biscuit how much was left and who got what: and he continued this function in the new arrangement, organizing the provisions that remained, calculating what fourteen men and a child and an uncertain number of sealed passengers would need to reach Quebec, rationing with the grim precision of a man who knew the numbers and respected them regardless of how he felt about the situation that produced them.

He did not speak about Moreau.

He did not speak much.

He communicated in the minimal language of practical men performing practical functions, and what he communicated was sufficient, and what he left out was everything, and everyone understood both halves.

Two of the men took the foremast watch in alternating shifts, not because the watch served any navigational function. It was clear to all that the ship did not require their eyes, nor respond to their calls, did not alter its heading based on anything they reported, but because the watch was a structure and the structure was something. They called out what they saw. They logged it in the watch book that Moreau had kept and that Renard maintained now; the entries growing sparser as the days passed and the entries became the same: Heading maintained. Wind sufficient. No incident.

No incident was the phrase Renard used. He had settled on it after the first day, when he had written the full account of the deck and crossed it out and wrote it again and crossed it out again and finally penned no incident and moved to the next line. The watch book was a document. Documents were read by people who had not been there. No incident was the entry that fit, the entry that served the log's function, the entry that maintained the fiction of a voyage rather than the truth of whatever this damnable walk through the shadow of death was.

He wrote no incident every watch and kept the log and waited for Quebec.

* * *

The possessed men were not a problem.

This was the second of unexpected things. Renard had braced for them as a threat, had positioned his fourteen men with an eye toward the possessed eight who moved through the ship with their easy, fluid lack of hesitation, and the possessed men had simply — continued. They maintained the ship with an efficiency that the original crew had not matched. They worked the rigging when the rigging required human hands for specific tasks, which was rare and became less frequent as the crossing progressed, as if the ship were gradually learning to do more on its own and needed them less. They ate from the provisions with the mechanical regularity of machines performing maintenance on themselves. They did not speak.

Nor did they bother the fourteen.

Renard tested this on the third day, positioning himself in the path of one of them: a man named Vidal who had been a competent deckhand and who was now...well now he was something that wore Vidal's body and did Vidal's work without being Vidal in any sense that mattered. The man had simply walked around him, accommodating the obstacle with the fluid indifference of water moving around a stone.

No aggression. No acknowledgment. No recognition.

Renard was nothing but mere furniture to them. The fourteen were furnishings, obstacles to be routed around, irrelevant. The ship was what mattered. The ship was what they served, tended to and inhabited, and the fourteen men standing on the deck looking at the horizon were simply part of the ship's contents, like the provisions and the ballast, present and accounted for and requiring no action.

This was better than what he had feared. Yet worse than anything he had a name for. The specific horror of being rendered moot by what had taken everything from you; of being left alive not because you had won but because you were not worth, the attention required to end you. A horror without a word in any language Renard knew, and he was a man who had been at sea for thirty years and had a wide vocabulary for horror.

He kept his watch.

And wrote, *No incident.*

* * *

Antoine came on deck twice a day.

He came at dawn and at dusk, in the thin light of the hours when the sky was neither fully dark nor fully bright, the transitional light that belonged to no clear category. He stood at the rail, always the starboard rail, always the same position, for precisely as long as it took him to survey the deck and the horizon and the condition of the ship and then went below again.

He did not speak to Renard directly. And if he did, he spoke in the manner a senior official speaks to a subordinate who is managing a situation adequately: a nod, occasionally a word that conveyed acknowledgment of the situation's management without engaging with the specifics of what was being managed. Renard received these communications with the expression of a man who had decided that the expression he wore was the last piece of himself he fully controlled and was controlling it with great care.

The Commandant did not speak to the possessed men.

Nor look at the faces in the deck planking.

He ate. He slept or performed the horizontal stillness of a man, allowing his body to do what it needed to do. He read his commission documents, which Renard had seen him doing once through the porthole of his berth, sitting at the small desk with the documents arranged before him and a lantern burning at his elbow, reading them with the focused attention of a man who had staked everything on what they contained and wanted to be certain they said what he needed them to say.

He kept the ledger.

Renard knew this because he had seen it: not the contents, not the names, but the book itself, sitting on Antoine's desk beside the commission documents, and Antoine's hand moving across a new page with the methodical attention of a man who was adding to an account rather than reviewing one. He was continuing it. The creature's ledger, the infernal invoice, the running account of what the de la Mothe name had cost and what its increasing tab, and Antoine was keeping the entries current, adding the crossing's names to the column with the same precision his grandmother's notation had applied to every name before them.

Renard did not ask about this. He did not have the question formed properly enough to ask it, and yet he suspected the answer would not improve his situation.

He kept his watch.

***

Marguerite was on deck every day.

She came up in the mornings when the light was strong and stayed until the evening when the light went, and she occupied the forecastle with the comfortable proprietorship of a child who had found a space that was hers and saw no reason to apologize for it. She sat on the rope coils and stood at the rail, and she walked the foredeck in the small circuits that children walk when they were thinking, and she talked.

The talking was both continuous and quiet, the low conversational murmur of someone engaged in a dialogue that required their full attention. She listened. She responded. She laughed occasionally, the genuine laugh of a child who had heard something that genuinely amused her, neither performed nor directed at anyone on deck, and then the conversation would resume.

The possessed men moved around her without altering their routes. The ship's rigging worked around her position without reference to it. She was not furniture to the ship in the manner the fourteen were furniture. She was something else. A guest. The guest of the thing that had made itself the ship, and the ship accommodated its guest with the easy hospitality of something that had chosen to be hospitable.

Renard watched her from the helm.

He had stopped trying to categorize what she was. He had spent the first days after the deck breathed working through the available categories — child, victim, instrument, conduit, something worse than any of these, and had arrived at the conclusion that the categories were not adequate and that applying inadequate categories to a situation was a form of dishonesty he couldn't afford. She was what she was. She was eight years old, and she talked to a thing that had killed men he knew, and the thing was gentle with her, and the gentleness was a choice, and he did not know what that choice meant, only that if demons could find something gentle in the world he had better be careful not to offend,. Lest the ire of the creature turn its eye towards him.

She called down to her mother every afternoon.

This was the part Renard could not stop thinking about. The afternoons when Marguerite went to the sealed hatch and crouched beside it and called down through the wood, and Céleste's voice came back up through the grain of the ship's new self, muffled and close, the particular quality of a voice heard through material that had absorbed it.

"Are you all right?" Céleste would ask.

"Yes, Mama," Marguerite would said. "Everything is fine."

And the ship. The thing in the ship, let her say this. Allowed it. Did not prevent the conversation, did not use the hatch as leverage, did not turn the communication into an instrument of anything. Just let the child talk to her mother through the wood and let the mother hear the child's voice and let both of them have their conversations without interference.

The thing was not cruel. Cruelty implied caring about the suffering of the other, implied a relationship with the other's experience, implied that the other's experience was the point. The thing was not interested in the suffering for its own sake. The suffering was incidental, a byproduct, much like a fire's heat is a byproduct of fire.

No, it was not cruel.

It was indifferent.

And indifference, Renard had concluded, was worse. Cruelty could be appealed to. Cruelty had a relationship with you, even if the relationship was terrible. Indifference held no relationship with you. Indifference was the fire, and you were simply the thing in its path.

Except for Marguerite.

Except for the child at the forecastle rail talking to something in the middle of the Atlantic, and the ship letting her call to her mother, and the gentleness that was a choice.

He had been thinking about this for days and had arrived nowhere useful with it, which meant either that there was no useful place to arrive or that he was not the right person to arrive there, and both of those possibilities led to the same place, which was keeping his watch and writing no incident and waiting for Quebec.

* * *

Below, the passengers maintained the litany.

Not continuously, not every waking hour, not through the nights when exhaustion finally overrode the fear and people slept in the fitful, shallow way of people sleeping in an enclosed space with something wrong: but regularly, structured, Sister Marie-Claire bringing them back to it when the silence had lasted long enough to fill with the other things that silence filled with.

She had taken the Litany as her function, Gros had taken the provisions, and Renard had taken the watch. It was what she had, and she determined to have it completely, to give it her all rather than performing it as a comfort, because performance in this situation would not save them. She had watched a priest perform his faith for eleven years, Eleven years of false piety. A falseness she did not perceive in her duration with the man. But a falseness clearly exposed in the common area when the child's hand had found Father Lescaut's wrist and his face had contorted.

He was dead, and she was not going to perform.

And the passengers said them with her.

Blanchard said them, which surprised Sister Marie-Claire when she noticed it. He had not struck her as a man of faith. He had struck her as a man of documents and procedures and the careful architecture of evidence, which she supposed was its own kind of faith but was not usually the kind that said the Litany in the dark of a ship's sealed hold. She had revised her assessment of him several times during the crossing and was revising it now again.

He was also writing.

He had been writing continuously. The small notebook, filled and supplemented with loose pages folded into it, his careful notary's hand recording the sequence of events with the precision of a legal document. He recorded the compass on day four. He recorded the trunk. He recorded the four dead men by name, which he had obtained from one of the sailors early in the crossing for reasons he had not explained and had not needed to explain. He recorded Lescaut's ministry and Lescaut's exposure, which he had not witnessed directly but had reconstructed from account and inference, and he noted the reconstruction and its sources as a proper document required.

He recorded the deck.

He had been at the porthole of the passenger berth's single small window when the deck breathed, positioned there by the accident of standing when the rest of the sealed passengers were trying the hatches, and he had seen what he had seen and he had written it in the notebook in his careful hand and had not crossed it out.

He had seen the faces.

He had not told the other passengers about the faces. He had told himself this was because they had enough to manage without that specific information, which was true, and because knowing would not help them, which was also true, and he was aware that there was a third reason which was that he could not say it aloud without it becoming real in a way that the notebook contained it from being, and for this third reason he did not write it down.

He recorded no incident in his notebook too, which was not what he wrote, but it was the same gesture as Renard's — the maintenance of a form in the absence of anything adequate to fill it.

The floor of the passenger compartment was warm.

The grain of the wood, which Simone Aubert had decided she would not look at and had maintained this decision with a rigidity that had become its own kind of strength, was what it was. She had organized her sons against the bulkhead farthest from the floor's interior planking and had created a small world within the sealed world of the berth: their blankets, their provisions allotted by Blanchard, the stories she told them at night when the Litany was done and the other adults had settled into their exhausted half-sleep.

The stories were the stories her mother had told her. The simple ones. The ones with good endings.

Her younger son had stopped asking about his father on the third day.

She did not know what this meant and was not going to examine it until she was in a position to act on what the examination revealed, which required getting off this ship, which required Quebec, which required the ship to arrive.

She told the stories.

Her elder son listened. Her younger son pressed his face into her side and she felt his breathing, which was the breathing of a child asleep, slow and regular and entirely real, and she held him and told the story and felt the floor warm beneath her and did not look at the grain of the wood.

***

On the sixth day after the deck breathed, Marguerite came down through the hatch.

This was new. She had been on deck every day and had called through the hatch to her mother every afternoon and had not come below, and the hatch had not opened for her or for anyone. Renard had tried it twice in the first days and found it as sealed as before and had stopped trying. But on the sixth day the hatch opened, and Marguerite came down the ladder with the simple confidence of a child coming home.

The sealed passengers looked at her.

She looked at them. At Sister Marie-Claire. At Blanchard. At the Aubert family against the bulkhead.

She went to her mother.

Céleste held her the way mothers hold children who have been apart from them: completely, without reservation, with the full weight of the days in the holding. Marguerite let herself be held. For a moment she was entirely eight years old, her face against her mother's shoulder, her arms around her mother's neck, the simple animal comfort of the reunion.

Then she straightened and looked around the berth.

She looked at the floor.

Her face, looking at the floor, was not the face of a child seeing something terrible. It was the face of the child at the forecastle rail: the patient, knowing face, the face that had been waiting since La Rochelle. She looked at the floor how someone looked at a thing they have known about for a long time and was now seeing it directly for the first time, confirming the accuracy of the description.

She looked at Simone Aubert.

Something moved through her face then, something genuine, something that was the face of a child looking at a mother and knowing what the mother did not know and carrying the weight of the knowing.

She did not say anything. She went back to her mother and sat beside her, and held her hand.

Blanchard looked at this and wrote something in his notebook.

Sister Marie-Claire looked at this and began the litany again, quietly, and the other passengers joined her.

The floor was warm.

The ship moved through the Atlantic with its beautiful, terrible efficiency, the rigging perfect, the heading true, the compass spinning freely yet meaning nothing, and the ship going where the hell it wanted, anyway.

* * *

On the morning of the ninth day after the deck breathed, Renard saw the shore.

He saw it the way you see shore after a long crossing — first as a quality of the light on the horizon, a density, a difference in how the air sat over that part of the water, and then as the thing itself, rising, becoming solid, becoming real in much as land becomes real after weeks of water.

He stood at the helm that did not need him and watched it rise.

He thought: Quebec.

He thought: God help them.

He thought about the people in the berth below. The Aubert woman telling stories, Sister Marie-Claire saying the Litany, the notary with his careful pages, and he thought about what they were sailing toward and what was coming into harbor behind the thing that was bringing them there.

He did not call out to the shore.

It seemed redundant. The ship knew where it was. The ship had always known where it was. The shore did not require his announcement.

He looked at the wheel, turning, steady.

He looked at the shore.

He wrote in the log: Land sighted. Quebec, approximately. ETA...

He stopped. He thought about the ETA. He thought about who determined it.

He crossed out ETA and wrote nothing after it and closed the log.

The ship sailed on toward the shore with, and the shore rose to meet it, and the faces looked up from the deck planking with their various expressions of the enormous, and the morning light fell on all of it without distinction, and somewhere in the forecastle Renard could see that Marguerite was talking to her friend about what happens next.

She nodded.

She knew.

Chapter Nineteen

The Fog

The fog came up from the river the way the St. Lawrence had always made fog: not from above, not descending like weather, but rising as if exhaled from the water itself, the river breathing out what the cold air above it could not hold. It came in the early morning of the day after Renard had seen the shore, and it was the kind of fog that was not a diminishment of visibility but a replacement of it, a substitution of one world for another, the world of distance and horizon and the ordinary geometry of water and sky replaced by a world of white that had no depth and no direction and no reference point except the deck under your feet and the mast above your head and the sound of the water against the hull, which the fog thickened and changed so that even that sound was not quite itself.

Renard stood at the helm in the white and could not see the bow.

He could not see twenty feet. He could not see the forecastle where Marguerite had spent the crossing talking to her friend. He could not see the mainmast from the helm, though he knew it was there and could put his hand on it if he walked eight steps forward, and he knew this intellectually, but the fog had done what fog does to intellectual knowledge, which was to make it feel insufficient.

He stood at the helm and listened.

The ship moved.

Not cautiously, not the careful slow-motion transit of a vessel feeling its way through fog, sounding its depth, watching its speed, the crew at the rail with poles and eyes straining for obstacles. The ship moved at the speed it had been making since the deck breathed, the purposeful, unhurried speed of something that knew its destination and held no concern about what lay between here and there because what lay between here and there presented no impediment to it.

The St. Lawrence had rocks. Every sailor who had made this crossing knew the St. Lawrence had rocks, knew the channels and the sandbars and the particular treacheries of the river traffic. The other vessels making the passage, the fishing boats working the closer banks, the supply ships and the traders and the indigenous canoes that moved through the river with a confident knowledge of its currents that took years to acquire. All of these things were in the fog with them. All of these things were in the path the ship was taking.

The ship moved through the fog, and nothing happened.

No collision. No grounding. No scrape of keel against the sand. The river traffic that should have been there was there. And the fog was not so absolute that Renard could not hear the voices carrying across the water, or the creak of other vessels' rigging, once the clear bell of another ship's foghorn at what sounded like a distance that should have been a collision: parted for them. He could hear things moving out of the way. He could hear the sound of water being displaced by something that was moving quickly to avoid the thing coming through the fog, and he could hear voices calling out in French and in languages he didn't know, the voices of people on other vessels encountering something on the river that was not making any of the sounds a vessel made when it was being careful in fog.

The ship made none of those sounds because the ship was not being careful.

The ship had not been careful since La Rochelle.

* * *

On the north bank, at the settlement of three houses that sat above the river on a limestone outcropping, a man named Théodore Marchand was splitting wood.

He had been splitting wood since before the fog came up, and the fog had not stopped him because the wood needed splitting and a man did not stop working because of weather on the St. Lawrence, where weather was the permanent condition and clear days were the exceptions you noted and were grateful for. He split wood in the fog and listened to the river like men who spent their lives beside rivers listened to rivers: not consciously, not with directed attention, but with the background receptivity of a person for whom the river's sounds were the baseline against which all other sounds were measured.

And Théodore Marchand heard the ship before he saw it.

Or rather, he heard the absence of what a ship made. He heard the displacement of water, the bow wave of something large moving through the river, and he did not hear the sails working or the crew calling or the pilot's instructions or any of the sounds that accompanied the displacement of water by a vessel with men on it. He merely heard the water moving around something, and he heard nothing else.

He put down the axe and walked to the bank to investigate.

The fog was thick enough that he could see perhaps thirty feet of river before the white consumed it, and for a long moment he saw nothing, just the white and the dark water surface and the fog lying on the water in the way fog lay on the water here, heavy, close, the fog of the St. Lawrence which was different from ocean fog in ways that men who knew both rivers and oceans understood and could not fully articulate to those who knew only one.

Then the ship came through the fog; ghostlike. Like a serpent ready to strike if agitated.

It came at a speed that was the wrong speed for the river and the wrong speed for the fog and the wrong speed for any vessel that was being navigated by men who understood that rocks and sandbars and other vessels existed and required consideration. But the frigate was not so. It moved at the speed of something that did not require consideration. A speed that, if it were a living thing, other living things knew to avoid.

Théodore Marchand stood on the bank and looked at it.

The hull first — dark, the wood of it wet and blackened by the crossing, the waterline sitting wrong in a way he could not immediately account for, too low, perhaps, or the trim was off, or the color of the wood was not the color of wood that had been through weather in the ordinary way. The hull came out of the fog and passed him, and the bow wave reached the bank and moved the bank's stones with a sound like breath.

Then the deck.

He looked at the deck.

Marchand was a man who had seen ships his whole life. He had been born on this river and had spent forty years watching vessels come up it and go down it, and he knew what a ship's deck looked like from the bank when a ship passed at this distance. He knew what the deck looked like with men on it, to see figures at the rail and at the mast and at the helm, the organized human presence that gave a ship its character, that made it a vessel rather than a floating object.

The deck had no men on it.

Or he corrected himself, squinting into the fog, because the fog did things to perception, and a man should be careful. The deck had almost no men on it. There was a figure at the bow. Small. The figure of a child, standing at the forecastle rail with its hands on the wood and its face pointed forward into the fog, the posture of a lookout who is not watching for obstacles but is simply facing the direction of travel, the way you face the direction of travel when you are arriving somewhere and want to be the first to see it.

And there was a figure at the midship rail. A man. Standing with his hands behind his back and his face turned toward the bank, toward the place where Théodore Marchand was standing, and for a moment, for the duration of the ship's passage, which was not long at the speed it was making. The figure on the deck and the man on the bank looked at one another across the fog-hazed water.

The man on the deck did not move. Did not acknowledge. Did not alter his posture or his expression, which Théodore could not read at this distance but which had the quality of composure, of a man standing where he had chosen to stand and finding the standing adequate.

The ship passed.

The fog closed in behind it.

Théodore Marchand stood on the bank and listened to the bow wave's stones settle back into their positions and listened to the sound of the displacement fading as the ship moved upriver, and then he went back to his wood and picked up the axe and stood with it for a long time without bringing it down.

Then he went inside and told his wife what he had seen.

She listened. She was a woman who had also lived on this river for forty years and who had heard many things about the river and who applied to all such accounts the same measured consideration, neither credulous nor dismissive, the epistemology of a woman who understood that the river was larger than any individual's experience of it and contained things that individual experience had not yet cataloged.

She asked him what the ship had looked like.

He described it. The wrong color of the hull. The wrong speed. The child at the bow. The man at the rail who looked at the bank without looking.

She crossed herself.

She told him to say nothing about it in the settlement.

He asked why.

Because some things, she said, were best met at their destination rather than followed to it.

He put the axe away and said nothing in the settlement.

* * *

At the next bend, where the river curved, and the current ran differently and the fog sat thinner for a stretch of perhaps two hundred yards, a group of Huron men in two canoes saw the ship.

They had been fishing since before the fog came up, working the bend where the currents change brought fish to the surface, and they knew this river with the comprehensive knowledge of people whose relationship with it preceded the settlement of anyone who arrived by ship. They knew the fog of this bend and how thick it ran and how thin, and they knew when the fog was thin enough to work and when it was not, and this morning it was thin enough and they tasked themselves to work.

They too heard the ship before they saw it, as Théodore had heard it. The wrong sounds, and the absence of the right sounds, the water moving around something large that was not making the sounds that large things made when men were in charge of their movement through the water.

The canoes held still.

The ship came around the bend.

They looked at it. They looked at the deck. They looked at the child at the bow and the man at the rail and the rigging that moved without hands in it and the helm that turned without a hand on it.

They looked at each other.

One of the men said something. The others listened. He said it again, pointing at the ship, and the others nodded in the manner of people confirming the accuracy of an identification: not *I have never seen this* but *I know what this is and I know its name and I know what it means that it is here.*

The ship passed them. Its bow wave rocked the canoes, and they held them without difficulty, as men who knew water held themselves in water.

They watched it go.

They did not follow it.

They paddled to the bank and pulled the canoes up, and they did not return to the river that day. That evening, at the fire, the man who had spoken first told the others what he had said, and they discussed it with the serious attention of people for whom certain categories of event required serious attention, and they reached a conclusion about what the ship was carrying and where it was going and what that meant for where it was going.

They sent a runner to the next settlement.

The runner was a young man who ran fast and who was told what to say and who said it at the next settlement, and the next settlement sent its own runner, and the message moved up the river faster than the ship, which was not difficult because the ship was moving at slow coast and messages moved at the speed that runners moved, and runners who knew the trail's path could move very quickly on it.

The message arrived at Quebec three hours before the ship.

* * *

On the deck, in the fog, Marguerite stood at the forecastle rail.

She had been there since the fog came up, which was before dawn, which meant she had been there in the dark first and then in the growing light that the fog converted into an even, directionless white, standing at the rail with her hands on the wood and her face pointed forward. She was not watching for anything. She did not need to watch. Robin knew where he was going and told her he was the captain of the ship, and therefore the ship knew where it was going, and she was privy to know where the ship was going, and the watching was not the point.

The point was being at the front of it.

She had always been at the forefront of it. She had been at the front of it since the dock at La Rochelle, when she had been the first thing Antoine encountered on the ship that was wrong in the way that everything after it would be wrong, the first note of a scale he could not yet hear but that she had already heard completely. She had handed him the ribbon. She had given him the luck, which was not luck in the ordinary sense but was the only word the transaction had in French.

She stood at the rail and felt the ship move under her, the breathing of it, the deep slow rhythm that was different from the mechanical rhythm of a vessel under sail and she felt it like you feel something you have always known the way you know your own breathing — present, constant, so familiar and below the level of attention.

She could feel Quebec ahead of them. Not see it. The fog removed seeing from the available options, but feel it, much like you feel a destination when you are close to it and have been traveling toward it for a long time. The quality of the air was different. The fog itself was different, thicker here than on the open water, the St. Lawrence's particular fog that came up from the river and sat on it with the possessive heaviness of something that had always been there and intended to remain.

She could feel the city.

She thought about what Robin had told her about the city. He had told her a great deal in the weeks of the crossing, in the conversations at the rail and in the hold and in the dark of the night when the ship breathed and she was the only person on the open deck. He had told her about the straits, which was where Antoine was going. The place where the lakes narrowed, and the water ran fast between them, the place that had been a significant place long before Antoine arrived to make it a significant place in the accounting of the French crown.

He had told her what he intended to do there.

She had listened with the attention she gave to everything he told her, which was complete, careful and without fear. She was not frightened of him. She had not been frightened of him since the first night, since the forecastle rail when he had appeared beside her and told her his name for himself, which was not Rouge-gorge, and she had told him her name for him, which she would keep, and he had accepted this with the pleasure of something that had not been named by something that was not afraid of it in a very long time.

The city grew in the fog ahead of them.

She could feel it growing. She could feel the pier and the quay and the officials with their documents and the soldiers with their weapons and the ordinary morning of a river city that had received a message three hours ago and was doing what cities do when they receive messages about ships that move without crew at the wrong speed in the wrong fog.

She could feel them waiting.

She thought about her mother below. She thought about Monsieur Cadillac at the midship rail with his documents and his composed face. She thought about Renard at the helm that did not need him, writing no incident in his log with the steady hand of a man who has decided that the doing of things is the last form of dignity available.

She thought about the faces in the deck planking and about what she knew and what she was not going to say to the men on the pier, and what was going to happen next, and what Robin had said about what was going to happen next, which was more than she was going to tell anyone on the pier and less than she already knew.

The fog began to thin.

Not lifting, not the dramatic revelation of fog burning off in morning sun, but thinning, gradually, the white becoming less absolute, shapes beginning to resolve within it, the shapes of buildings on a height above the river, the shapes of other vessels at their moorings, the shapes of men on a pier who had received a message and were standing at the end of it looking out into the fog at the sound of something coming.

Marguerite watched the city emerge from the white.

She put her hands on the rail and looked at it. The limestone heights and the wooden buildings and the flag and the soldiers and the pier with its men, and she felt the ship move toward it with its beautiful, terrible efficiency, and she felt Robin all around her, in the wood under her hands and the deck under her feet and the rigging above her head, and she felt his pleasure, which was the pleasure of arrival, which was the pleasure of something that has been traveling for a very long time and had now reached the place it was traveling toward.

Not the end.

The beginning.

The fog thinned further.

Quebec came clear.

The ship came out of the fog and into the morning, moving at the speed it had been making, and on the pier the men who had been waiting in the fog saw it come out and saw the deck and saw the child at the forecastle rail and the man at the midship rail and the rigging moving without hands and the helm turning without a hand, and they stood on the pier with all of that in front of them and did what men do when they encounter something that exceeds their category of possible experiences.

Some of them called out.

The ship did not respond.

Some of them crossed themselves.

The ship came in.

Chapter Twenty

The Port

The ship found the quay the way it had found everything since the deck breathed — without hesitation, without the careful incremental approach of a vessel under human navigation, without the pilot that Quebec required of every ship entering the harbor and that the harbormaster had been attempting to dispatch since the message arrived three hours ago and that had not been dispatched because no pilot had been willing to go out into the fog toward a ship that moved the way the messages described this ship moving.

It came in at the speed it had been making, and then it did not.

The deceleration was not gradual: not the slow bleed of speed that happened when a vessel came off the river current into the harbor's sheltered water, not the managed reduction of sail, not any of the mechanisms that produced the approach of a ship under human management. The speed simply resolved, as a held note resolves, from the crossing speed to the harbor speed to the quay speed in a transition that took perhaps forty seconds and that the harbormaster's watching from the stone wall above would describe afterward in terms that contradicted each other because they had all seen something different and all of them were right.

The lines went out on their own.

Not thrown: extended, the mooring lines running out from the cleats as if pulled from below the quay rather than from above it, finding the bollards with the precision of something that had done this before, had done it many times, had done it on this specific quay at this specific berth in a previous arrangement that the current arrangement was simply recapitulating. The lines drew taut. The ship stopped moving. The fenders, which had been in their storage positions since the crossing began and had not been rigged because there was no one rigging them; were against the quay, holding the hull at the correct distance, sitting exactly where fenders needed to sit when a ship was making fast.

The harbormaster, whose name was Claude Beaumont and who had been managing this quay for fourteen years, a man who had seen ships come in under every conceivable condition of weather and emergency and human incompetence, stood on the quay and looked at what the ship had just done to his bollards and said nothing for a long time.

His assistant, standing beside him, said: "How did it..."

"I don't know," Beaumont said.

"Should we..."

"I don't know," Beaumont said again. He was still looking at the lines. They were correctly tied. They were correctly tensioned. They were more correctly tied and tensioned than most pilots managed in good conditions in full daylight with a full crew, and they had been tied and tensioned by nothing he could see.

He looked at the ship.

The fog was still present over the water but thinner here, in the harbor, the morning light began to work through it in the way it worked through the St. Lawrence's fog — slowly, without drama, the white becoming translucent and then transparent in patches, the patches expanding, the city emerging in pieces. The ship sat in the thinning fog, and the thinning fog showed it to the assembled men on the quay in increments, which was worse than showing it all at once would have been. The hull first, the dark wood of it, the wrong color they had been warned about in the messages, the waterline sitting just as it was sitting; then the deck, which the fog had not yet cleared entirely but which showed enough; then the rigging, motionless now, hanging slack after the efficiency of the approach, hanging as rigging hung on a ship at rest.

A ship at rest with no one on it.

Or the fog had not cleared entirely. There were figures. Beaumont could see figures on the deck, shapes in the white that resolved, as the fog continued to thin, into the forms of men. Not moving. Not at the lines they had just tied, nor at the helm they had just brought in, or at any of the positions that men occupied when they had just completed a docking. Simply standing. Or not standing. He could not fully resolve the shapes, the fog still too thick for the details, but they were there, on the deck, occupying the deck in numbers that were wrong for a vessel this size, too few, far too few, and arranged in positions that were not the positions of men who had just finished working.

He looked at the gangplank.

The gangplank extended.

Not thrown out, not carried and placed but extended, sliding out from the ship's side with the smooth mechanical efficiency of a thing that knew what it was doing, finding the quay's edge and settling onto it with the precision of something that had measured the gap and accounted for it. It rested on the quay stone with a solidity that communicated permanence; this gangplank was down and would be down, and the distance between the ship and the quay had been bridged and the bridge was real and anyone who intended to use it should use it.

Beaumont looked at the gangplank on his quay.

He looked at his men. The dozen workers who had come to the quay when the message arrived, the four soldiers who had been stationed here since the runner came in and whose officer had positioned them at the gangplank's potential landing point with the practical instinct of a man who did not know what was coming but had decided to put armed men between himself and it. He looked at the small crowd that had gathered behind the soldiers, the workers and merchants and early risers and people who had heard the messages and the messages about the messages and had come to the quay because people came to quays when something was arriving that was larger than the ordinary business of arrival.

He looked at the gangplank.

He looked at the ship.

***

Antoine came down first.

He came down the gangplank as he had come down every gangplank in his career: with the deliberate, unhurried step of a man of some official standing descending to ground that a man of his standing had already claimed, the step that communicated, I know where I am and I know who I am and both of those things are in order. His coat was on and buttoned correctly. His documents were under his left arm in the leather case he had carried since La Rochelle, the case worn at the corners from the handling it had received during the crossing but intact, the contents intact, the commission and the patents and the letters of instruction all present and in the order in which they would need to be presented.

His face was the face.

The composed face, the face that had been looking out from behind his eyes since the hold where Father Lescaut's book had closed and the ritual had not completed and the pact had been renewed. The face of a man managing a complex enterprise and encountering an unexpected logistical development and yet proceeding. The face that had looked at Renard in the passage and told him the trunk was to be moved to his quarters. The face that had stood at the mainmast while the deck breathed and held a small hand and looked at the city in his mind.

He reached the quay.

He looked at Beaumont. He looked at the soldiers. He looked at the assembled crowd behind them with the assessing eye of a man who has arrived somewhere and is taking stock.

Then he looked at the men behind the soldiers, The merchants and the workers and the curious, and something moved through his face that was there and gone before most of them registered it, a shadow of the thing that should have been there, the thing that had been there briefly in the hold with the stole folded and the stole's folding meaning nothing now, the thing that came and went and left no trace except its coming.

Gone.

He straightened his documents.

He looked at Beaumont and said, in the voice of a man who has arrived after a long journey and had things to do: "Antoine de la Mothe Cadillac, Commandant, expedition to establish Fort Pontchartrain du Détroit, bearing a commission from Minister Pontchartrain dated..."

"Monsieur," Beaumont said. He was still looking at the ship. "What has happened to your—where is your crew? Where is your captain? Where are the..."

"There was illness aboard," Antoine said. "Severe and unusual. The captain and several of the crew were lost. I will provide a full accounting to the officials in the appropriate sequence." He produced the top document from the case and presented it. "My commission. I would ask that you verify it and direct me to the Governor's representative."

Beaumont looked at the document. He looked at Antoine. He looked at the document again.

He was a man of procedure. Procedure was his function and his identity and the framework through which he understood his responsibility, and the document in front of him was a real document, correctly issued, correctly sealed, the kind of record that his procedure required him to process in the way that his procedure specified. Everything about the document was in order.

Everything about the man presenting it was not.

He took the document.

* * *

Marguerite came down behind Antoine.

She descended the gangplank with the careful stepping of a child navigating a steep surface, both hands on the rope guide, her traveling cloak around her shoulders, her dark braid catching the morning light that was now coming through the thinning fog with some conviction. She reached the quay and looked up at the assembled men and the soldiers and the crowd behind the soldiers with the expression of a child who has arrived somewhere after a long journey and is assessing the arrival.

She found Antoine's hand.

He let her take it.

The crowd looked at the child. The crowd had been told — the message had said a man and a child — but the message had not conveyed this specific quality of the child standing on the quay holding the commandant's hand, looking at them with that expression. The expression that was not a child's expression and had not been since La Rochelle. The patience of it. The waiting.

Several people in the crowd crossed themselves without deciding to. It was the reflexive crossing of people whose bodies had registered something before their minds could fully process it, the gesture that precedes the thought, the instinct engaging before the analysis.

Marguerite looked at them with that expression.

She looked at a soldier near the front whose face had gone pale, and she looked at him with something that was not hostility and was not warmth but was the complete attention of something that has noted your presence and will remember it.

The soldier took a step back.

She looked at Beaumont.

Beaumont looked back at her and found, to his considerable surprise, that he could not hold the look. There was nothing in the child's face that should have made looking away necessary. There was nothing hostile, or threatening, or supernatural about a small girl in a traveling cloak with a dark braid, standing on a quay in the morning fog, holding a man's hand. There was nothing in the look itself.

There was something behind the look.

He looked at his document.

***

The woman appeared at the top of the gangplank.

The fog was still present at the ship's deck level, thinner than it had been but still there, and she stood in it similar to how figures stand in fog: partially resolved, the edges of her uncertainty, the details dependent on the light finding its way through the white. She was dressed in the clothes of a woman who had been at sea for several weeks. The clothes were intact, were correct, were the clothes of a woman of ordinary means making a colonial crossing. She was holding the gangplank's rope guide with one hand and she was looking down at the quay with the expression of a woman who has emerged from a difficult ordeal and is composing herself on the threshold of arrival, and her expression was composed and her bearing was composed and everything about her was the expression of a woman who had survived something and intended to continue surviving it.

She called down.

"Hurry," she said. Her voice was clear and carried easily in the fog-dampened air of the harbor, the voice of a woman conveying important practical information to people who needed to have it. "There are people sealed in the decks below. They need to come out. Please send men up... there are passengers, they have been sealed below decks, they are alive and they need assistance."

The voice was helpful. Solicitous. The voice of someone whose concern was for the other passengers, whose own discomfort was secondary to the practical necessity of getting the information conveyed to the people who could act on it.

The soldiers looked at their officer.

The officer looked at the woman on the gangplank.

He looked at her, and something in his gaze snagged, the way looking snags when the eye has registered something that the mind is still processing. How you look at an object and know something is wrong about it before you have identified what. He looked at her and she looked back at him and her face was the face it had been: composed, helpful, concerned, the face of a woman who wanted the sealed passengers freed and was directing the people with the authority to free them — and her eyes, when the morning light came through the fog at the angle it came through at that moment, at the specific angle of early morning light over the St. Lawrence harbor finding its way through thinning fog onto the face of a woman standing at the top of a gangplank ...

Her eyes were the wrong color.

Not dramatically. Not the full burning red of the thing in the hold, not the red of iron pulled from a forge. Just — wrong. Just the particular wrong of a color that was not the color that eyes were. A warmth in them that was not the warmth of brown and was not the warmth of amber and was not any color that the officer could name, a color that was almost right and yet not right, a color that the morning light had briefly caught and revealed and that was already, as he watched, resolving back into the ordinary brown that it had been a moment ago.

He kept looking.

The color was gone. Brown eyes. Ordinary. Concerned and helpfully directing him to the sealed passengers below decks.

He looked at his men.

He looked at the gangplank.

He looked at the woman.

He was a soldier, and soldiers went where they were sent. He had been sent to this quay to manage the arrival of an unusual vessel, and he was managing it. The document was real. The commandant was on the quay. There were apparently passengers sealed below who needed to come out.

"You four," he said to the men nearest him. "Up the gangplank. Find the sealed passengers. Bring them out."

The four men looked at the ship. They looked at the gangplank. They looked at the woman at the top of it, who smiled at them with her ordinary brown eyes and stepped to the side to let them pass with the helpful efficiency of someone clearing the path.

They went up.

* * *

Céleste watched them come aboard.

She was standing at the top of the gangplank in the position she had come to when the hatch had opened — finally, suddenly, without ceremony, the wood releasing its hold like a hand releases when it is done holding, and the passengers had come up into the gray morning and found the fog and the quay and the gangplank already extended and Quebec already present in the thinning white.

She had come to the gangplank top because someone needed to be there to tell the quay what was needed, and she had told them, and they were sending men, and the men were coming up, and this was good, this was the practical outcome she had been directing toward.

She watched the four soldiers come up the gangplank toward her and she smiled and stepped aside and one of them looked at her and looked away quickly in the way that one of them had done, and she did not think about why, and she watched them go past her onto the deck and she turned to look at the quay.

Below, Antoine was talking to a man with documents. Marguerite was beside him. Her daughter was beside him, holding his hand, looking at the crowd on the quay with that expression she had been wearing since before La Rochelle, before Céleste understood what the expression was, and which Céleste now...

She stopped.

She looked at Marguerite.

Marguerite looked up at her from the quay.

And something passed between them — mother and daughter, the look between them, the look that had passed between them ten thousand times in eight years, the specific look of a mother and a child who know each other completely, who have no barriers between their understanding of each other, who have been in proximity long enough and in love long enough that the look is not communication so much as contact.

The look passed between them.

Marguerite held it.

And in the holding there was something that Céleste had not seen in her daughter's eyes before. Not the creature's red — not that, of that she was certain, she would have known that she had looked at those eyes through fog and darkness and fear for weeks, and she knew what they contained. Not the red.

Something else. Something warm. Something that was her daughter's and was also not only her daughter's, a warmth that was larger than one pair of eight-year-old eyes could account for, a warmth that had depth in it, that had age in it, that had patience in it.

That had been here before.

That was intended to be here again.

Céleste stood at the top of the gangplank in the early morning fog over the St. Lawrence and looked at her daughter's eyes and understood something that she was not going to be able to unlearn, something that had been true since the dock at La Rochelle and that she had been not understanding with great commitment and considerable skill for the entire crossing.

Marguerite smiled at her.

Her daughter's smile. Completely, entirely, her daughter's smile. The gap where the front tooth had been, the manner in which the left side came up slightly faster than the right, the smile she had been smiling since she was two years old and that Céleste knew as she knew her own name.

"Hurry, Maman," she called up. Her voice was her voice. Clear and carrying and entirely her own. "They need to know about the people below."

Céleste looked at her daughter.

She looked at the quay. At the soldiers coming up the gangplank past her toward the sealed hatches. At the harbormaster with his documents. At the crowd gathering, more of them now, the word having moved through the city with the speed that words about unusual ships moved through port cities.

She looked at Antoine, standing at the quay stone with his commission and his composed face. "Mossier Cadillac, I would like to assist Dr. Mercer with Mr. Fontaine. Can you watch Marguerite for a moment? She is clearly fond of you. I can find you within the hour."

Antoine looked at her and nodded. "Oui, mademoiselle, consider it of no import. You can find us with the governor."

Céleste smiled thankfully, then looked at her daughter with the unspoken look that signaled to a child that they should behave themselves.

She called down to the soldiers: "There are passengers below in the forward berth. The hatches may be difficult. There are also..." she stopped. She thought about what she was going to say. She thought about the deck. About the faces in the planking that she had not looked at and had known were there. About the names, she did not know. About Auber's daughters, whose names she had never asked.

"There are also others," she said. "In the deck. You will need..." she stopped again. "You will need to be careful."

The soldiers were already past her. She heard them on the deck, their boots on the planking, and she heard them stop, and she heard the quality of their stopping, which was the quality of boots stopping when the feet inside them have registered something through the soles that the feet were not prepared to register.

She heard one of them say something to another.

She did not hear what.

She looked at her daughter once more, then turned to head towards the passenger berths.

Marguerite was looking at the crowd on the quay. At the people crossing themselves. At the harbormaster with his document. At the city above the harbor on its limestone height, emerging from the fog in the morning light, becoming real, becoming what it was: a city, a functioning human city, full of ordinary people doing ordinary things in the ordinary way, a city that had received a message three hours ago and had sent soldiers and a harbormaster to the quay and had no idea, no framework, no category for what had just arrived in its harbor.

A city that was a beginning, not an end.

Marguerite stood on the quay in her traveling cloak and held Antoine's hand and looked at the city with the expression she had been wearing since La Rochelle.

Waiting.

Arriving.

Already thinking about Detroit.

***

Behind them, on the ship, the four soldiers had found the forward hatch and had found it opening under their hands. The wood releasing now; the ship done with its holding, the mechanism of the hatch working as it had been built to work, and they had gone down and they found the passengers.

The passengers came up into the morning light in as people come up when they have been in the dark for a long time and have not fully believed they might ever come up: blinking, pale, holding each other and holding the ladder rails and emerging onto a deck that they had heard do what it had done and that they were now standing on, and the standing on it was its own extraordinary thing, the deck solid and real and simply a deck, the morning light on it the same as the morning light that fell on everything.

Sister Marie-Claire came up third. She stood on the deck and looked at the sky. The real sky, the fog-diffused morning sky of the St. Lawrence, and moved her lips in something that was not the Litany and was not addressed to anyone she could name.

Blanchard came up fifth. He had his notebook. He stood on the deck and looked at it and looked at the quay and looked at his notebook again and wrote something, and whatever he wrote he wrote with the care of a man who wanted to get it exactly right because getting it exactly right is all he had.

Simone Aubert came up with her sons.

She came onto the deck and she looked at the deck and she saw what was in the deck and she saw what she had not let herself look at through the floor of the sealed berth and she looked at it and her face did not change in much like it did not change when she had said he's working to her younger son in a steady voice; the change happening behind the face rather than in it.

She looked at the deck.

She looked for a long time.

Then she took her sons' hands and walked them across the deck toward the gangplank, and she walked across the faces in the wood, and she did not look down.

Her younger son looked down.

She pulled his hand.

"Look at the water," she said. "Look at the river. We're here. We're in Quebec."

He looked at the river.

He let his mother lead him off the ship.

At the gangplank's top, Céleste stepped aside for them, and Simone passed her, and their eyes met for a moment. The eyes of two mothers who had been in the sealed berth together for the length of the worst crossing either of them would ever make, and what passed between them was not words and was not the Litany and was not anything that had a name but was entirely sufficient, the communication of people who have been through something together that they will never be able to explain to anyone who was not there.

Simone took her sons down the gangplank.

On the quay, in the morning light, her younger son turned to look back at the ship.

Marguerite was looking at him.

She lifted a hand. A child's wave, uncomplicated, direct, the wave of a child saying goodbye to another child, the simple gesture of an ordinary farewell.

He lifted his hand back.

His mother pulled him gently toward the city, and he went, looking back once more, and Marguerite was still looking at him with her hand up and the gap-toothed smile and the expression behind the smile that he was nine years old and did not have the categories for.

He turned and walked with his mother into Quebec.

***

Beaumont had the document.

He stood on the quay with Antoine's commission in his hands and the ship behind him and the morning continuing its work on the fog, and he processed the document because the document required processing and he was the harbormaster and the harbormaster processed documents.

The commission was real. The seals were correct. The authorization was clear. Antoine de la Mothe Cadillac, Commandant, expedition to establish Fort Pontchartrain du Détroit, bearing full authorization of the Minister Pontchartrain, was exactly what the document said he was.

He looked at the commandant.

Antoine met his eyes with the composed face.

"The Governor's representative," Antoine said again. "If you would direct me."

Beaumont looked at the ship. At the lines on his bollards, correctly tied. At the passengers coming down the gangplank, pale and blinking. At the soldiers who had come down behind the passengers and were speaking to their officer in low urgent voices and gesturing at the deck and the officer was listening with the expression of a man receiving information that is going to require a great deal of careful handling.

He looked at the child, standing beside the commandant, holding his hand, looking at the city.

He looked at the commandant.

"This way," he said.

He led Antoine off the quay and into the city and Marguerite went beside him, her hand in his, her face forward, looking at the city that was not where this ended.

Behind them, on the ship, the soldiers worked.

The fog continued to thin.

The morning continued.

And in the grain of the wood of the deck of La Vigilante, in the seams between the planks and the knots in the timber and the lines of growth that told the story of every tree the ship had ever been, the faces looked up at the sky with their various expressions of the enormous, and the morning light fell on them, and the river moved around the ship, and the city went about its morning, and none of it was what it had been before the ship arrived.

None of it would ever be again.

Chapter Twenty-One

A journey's end

The fog was still on the water, but the city was real above it.

Quebec sat on its limestone height as it had always sat — permanent, indifferent to the business of the harbor below it, the business of arrivals and departures and the administrative machinery that processed them, and the morning light was doing what morning light did on the St. Lawrence, working through the white from the east with the patient incrementalism of light that had been doing this every morning for longer than the city had been there to receive it.

Antoine stood on the quay with his documents inside his coat and watched the ship.

It floated against the quay the way ships floated. Inert. Wooden. The lines on the bollards holding it where it had placed itself, the hull moving with the small movements of a vessel in harbor water, the rise and fall of the river's breathing, the ordinary physics of displacement and buoyancy ebbing and flowing without the intervention of anything beyond themselves. The rigging hung slack. Nothing moved on the deck. No hand at the helm, no figure at the rail, no red eyes in the shadow of the hold — nothing. The ship was a ship. It floated against his quay, and it was a ship.

He had been watching it for ten minutes, and in all that time it had been a ship for all of them.

And yet he did not trust it. He did not trust the stillness of the hold in the early mornings of the crossing, the mornings when the banging had stopped and the box had been opened and the planking had been warm and everything had been quiet. He neither trusted the ship the way he had not trusted the quiet, which was not the absence of something but the presence of something that had finished with a particular thing and had moved on to the next thing, and the next thing was not there.

For him, the next thing was west. The straits and the rapids and the place where two great lakes narrowed between two shores and the water ran fast and cold between them, the place that existed in royal dispatches and in his own mind with the particular solidity of a thing he had been moving toward his entire adult life.

The next thing was Detroit.

He knew it was already thinking about Detroit because he was already thinking about Detroit, and the thinking and the things thinking had become, somewhere in the weeks of the crossing, difficult to distinguish from one another. He thought about the city and the years he waited to stamp his mark upon the world, waiting was what everything had been for, that the ledger had been for, that the pact renewed had been for, that Father Lescaut life had been for. The city at the straits, the fort, the settlement, the future that had his name on it.

His name.

He wondered how many would have to die to bring his dream to fruition. How many more families' fortunes would be transferred to enlarge his own? How many more faces would haunt his dreams now as he ledger'd away their lives to advance his own? Would he too die insane?

He straightened his coat.

Antoine had now been named twice.

It did not matter. He would update the ledger as he saw fit. He would identify those who would benefit him and his posterity, and he would list them throughout his life, until and if he determined that his role as this damned infernal record keeper of a malevolent bargain would cease with nail-scarred hands. He might turn from this path one day.

But not this day.

The trunk sat on the quay behind him.

He had hired the two men on the dock: workers, large, uninterested in what they were carrying, hired for their backs rather than their curiosity, and they had brought the trunk off the ship with the same almost-careful handling that all men gave it, the handling that was not rough and was not gentle and occupied the precise middle ground of men who did not want to be more in contact with a thing than the job required.

It sat on the quay stone, and nobody touched it uninstructed.

The workers stood at a distance that was slightly greater than the distance workers normally stood from the things they had been hired to carry. They were not consciously doing this. If asked, they would not have been able to account for the distance. They simply stood where they stood, and the trunk sat where it sat, and the quay stone between them was cold and wet from the fog and entirely ordinary.

Antoine looked at the trunk.

Dark wood with iron fittings and a brass clasp that was closed. A large traveling trunk of the kind that a man of official standing carried on a colonial crossing, worn at the corners from handling and dark with the moisture of weeks at sea. A simple trunk. On a quay. In the morning.

He looked at it for a long time.

He thought about the ledger inside it. The names going back to 1623, Édouard's farming family in Gascony, the first entry in a hand that was not human but was perfectly legible, and all the names that came after them, and the new names he had added in the days of the crossing's end in his own careful hand. He had added them because either he or the demon would ensure they were properly noted. Because the ledger existed, and the names were real, and the families they belonged to deserved to be in the accounting, even if the accounting was an infernal one, even if being in the accounting meant only that something kept track of the cost.

He thought about the commission inside his trunk. The authorization. The future in royal ink and ministerial seal.

He thought about his grandmother's box: the iron nails and the vial of salt and the bone-handled knife, and the folded paper in her hand, the paper he had read and understood and had understood was true and had chosen, anyway.

He looked at the trunk for the last time.

He then looked away.

The soldiers' voices came from inside the ship.

Urgent, overlapping, the voices of men encountering things they did not have training for and were managing with the tools they had, which were the voices of authority and the instinct to organize and the bodies of healthy young men who could carry other people if carrying was what was required. They had gone below and they were following orders as directed: orders followed with the focused competence of people who had not been told enough to be afraid of the ship.

Yet.

He could hear, underneath the soldiers' voices, the other sounds. Their appealing to the mother of God. Occasional vomiting by what they saw. The sounds of the passengers coming up. The specific quality of footsteps on a ladder when the person descending is managing themselves carefully, one rung at a time, holding on with both hands. He heard Sister Marie-Claire before he saw her: her voice, steady, leading someone else up, the calm authority of a woman who had said the Litany through the worst of it and had come out the other side still saying it.

She emerged at the top of the gangplank and came down and stepped onto the quay and stood on solid ground and looked at it.

She looked at it how you look at something you are certain you would not want to see again. Then she looked up. At the city. At the limestone height and the buildings and the flag and the ordinary, irreplaceable fact of a place where people lived and worked and went about the business of being alive.

She closed her eyes.

Her lips moved.

He could not hear what she said. It was not the Litany. It was something smaller and more direct, the words of a woman talking to God without the architecture of the formal prayer around it, just the words, the plain words of a specific woman in a specific moment with specific things to say to her Maker.

He looked away from her.

Blanchard came down the gangplank behind her, his notebook under his arm, his careful face set in the expression of a man who has arrived somewhere and intends to file a report and is already composing it. He stepped onto the quay and looked at Antoine.

Antoine looked back.

The look between them lasted a long time. Long enough for everything in it to be said without being said, which was all it would ever be. The things in that look were not things that could be said in any document or report or accounting, they were not words that Blanchard's notary's precision could get around or into or through; they were simply the things that were true between two men who had been on the same ship and could never fully share what that meant with anyone who had not been there.

Blanchard looked at him.

He looked at the notebook under his arm.

He looked at Antoine again.

He said quietly: "I have written it down."

"I know," Antoine said.

"All of it," Blanchard said. "The names. The dates. What happened to them." A pause. "What I heard you say in the hold."

Antoine held his eyes. "Yes."

"Someone should know," Blanchard said. It was not an accusation. It was not a threat. It was the statement of a notary — of a man who had dedicated his life to the proposition that the record mattered, that accuracy mattered, that the thing witnessed deserved to be written by someone whose function was to write things down.

"Yes," Antoine said again.

Blanchard looked at him for one more moment. Then he walked off the quay and into the city and did not look back, and Antoine watched him go and thought about the notebook and the names in it and the careful hand that had put them there, and he thought about what happened to notebooks, about what happened to documents, about the machinery of colonial administration and the ease with which inconvenient records found their way into the places where inconvenient things went. Antoine had determined that Blanchard was now an inconvenience.

He thought about this clearly and practically and without shame.

He thought I will need to speak to the Governor's office today. And will update the ledger with Blanchard's name.

He then put the thought away.

Simone Aubert came down with her sons.

She came down the gangplank with one boy on each side of her and her hands on both of them, and her face forward. Her face had been forward through the entire sealed dark of the berth, and she stepped onto the quay and kept moving because stopping was not the option, stopping was the thing she was not going to do until her sons were somewhere that was not a dock at the end of the crossing that had just ended.

She passed Antoine.

She did not look at him.

Her elder son looked at him as he passed. Fourteen years old, old enough to have understood more than his mother had allowed him to see, old enough to have heard things through the sealed hatch that she had not been able to prevent him from hearing, old enough to recall the account of the crossing in the manner that young people do the accounting of things, adding up what he had witnessed against what he had been told and finding the sum uncomfortable and not knowing yet what to do with the discomfort.

He looked at Antoine with the look of a young person who has not yet decided what face to wear for the thing they are looking at.

Antoine met the look.

The boy looked away and kept walking with his mother and his brother and did not look back.

The younger one looked back.

He was nine, and he was looking for Marguerite.

Céleste was not at the top of the gangplank.

She had been there, or there had been a figure there, a woman's figure in the fog with a helpful voice telling the soldiers about the sealed passengers, with ordinary brown eyes that had been ordinary brown except for the moment when the morning light had found them at the wrong angle. She had been there and now she was not there, and Antoine stood on the quay and looked at the top of the gangplank where she had been and calculated the possibilities.

She had gone back inside.

The fog had taken her.

She had never been there the way he understood there to work.

All three were possible. None of them were the thing he was going to investigate right now because Beaumont was coming back across the quay with the expression of a man who has been to find his superior and has found his superior and has explained the situation and has been told to return and manage it and is managing it, and the managing of it required Antoine's attention.

He gave it his attention.

He straightened his coat.

He looked down at Marguerite.

She had been beside him through all of it: through Blanchard's look and Sister Marie-Claire's prayer and Simone Aubert's passage and the younger boy looking for her, whom she had found with her eyes and waved to with the child's wave that was entirely her own. She had been beside him as she had been beside him since the deck breathed, her hand in his, her face taking in the quay and the city and the arrivals with the patient attention of something that has come to a destination after a long journey and is not in a hurry about what comes next.

She looked up at him.

Her eyes were the same dark eyes. The eyes from the dock at La Rochelle: patient, knowing, watching him with the particular quality of attention that had nothing of performance in it, it was simply there, completely, like the river was simply there and the fog was simply there and the morning was simply there. The eyes that had been watching him since the ribbon, since the luck that was not luck in the ordinary sense.

He looked at her.

He looked at her much as he had not looked at anything on the crossing: without the composed face, without the management of the looking, without the fraction of distance that he maintained between himself and everything he looked at, the distance that had allowed him to drive a nail through a priest's palm and turn away from the sounds that followed.

He looked at her directly.

She returned his gaze.

And her eyes changed.

Not gradually. Not the uncertain, almost-change that he had seen in Céleste's eyes at the top of the gangplank, the warmth that might have been the light. This was definite. This was the thing itself, the color that was not the color that eyes were, the red of iron pulled from a forge, the red of something that produced its own light because it had no need of borrowed light: two points of it, looking up at him from a child's face, warm and knowing and entirely without malice.

It was warm.

That was the thing he had not fully reckoned with in all the weeks of the crossing, in all the times he had seen it through a porthole or in the hold or at the stern in the pre-dawn gray. It was warm. Not the warmth of cruelty, not the warmth of appetite satisfied, not the warmth of something that had taken what it wanted and was pleased with the taking. The warmth of recognition. The warmth of a thing that knew him completely, knew him how the ledger knew the names, and how the crossing knew the water, and found the knowing sufficient, found Antoine de la Mothe Cadillac, in all his completeness and his failure and his city, and his ledger and his composed face, sufficient for the purpose.

The warmth of a thing that had been waiting for him since before he existed.

The warmth of a thing that was going to be waiting for him after he was gone.

He held the look.

The red was gone.

Her own dark eyes again. Eight years old. The gap-toothed smile. The traveling cloak. The braid.

She squeezed his hand.

"Robin says thank you," she said. The clear, carrying voice of a child who has a message and is making sure she gets it right. "He says he is going to look for any of his brethren, but he will be near should you need him, otherwise, he said he will see you in Detroit."

Antoine looked at her.

He thought about what thank you meant when the thing saying it was as old as when God populated Heaven and had gotten exactly what it had been working toward for at least three generations. He thought about the city at the straits and the founding and the patent and the commission inside his coat, and he thought about the shadow that his grandmother's letter had promised if he were to one day choose to renegotiate — his name synonymous with misfortune, history's unkind treatment, the things he built outlasting him and not remembering him well, and he thought about all of this looking down at a child who was eight years old and had a gap-toothed smile and had held his hand on a ship while the deck breathed.

He thought... He's welcome.

He did not say this.

He looked at the ship one more time. At the gangplank and the quay and the soldiers coming down it now with the last of the passengers, the stragglers, the ones who had needed more time to manage the ladder or the gangplank or the simple fact of the morning air after the sealed dark. They came down pale and blinking and wrapped their arms around themselves against the cold, and they stepped onto the quay and stood on solid ground, and most of them did not look back at the ship.

Renard came down last.

He came down the gangplank in the manner he had done everything on the crossing: with the steady deliberateness of a man who is doing what he has decided to do and has decided it completely. He stepped onto the quay, and he looked at the quay for a moment, at the stone of it, real and permanent and cold under his boots. Then he looked up.

He looked at Antoine.

And Antoine looked at Renard.

The look between them was longer than the look with Blanchard and contained different things. Blanchard had witnessed him. Renard had watched him be witnessed. Renard had stood at the helm for weeks and written no incident in the log and kept the count and kept the watch and kept the institution alive through the mechanism of his own refusal to stop keeping it, and Renard had done all of this with the full knowledge of what Antoine had done in the hold and what it had cost and what it was going to continue to cost.

Renard looked at him.

He did not say anything.

He took the watch log from under his arm. The book he had kept since Moreau died, the no incident log, the record of the crossing from the point when it stopped being a crossing in the ordinary sense, and he held it for a moment and he looked at it and then he looked at the river, and he dropped it in.

It hit the water and floated for a moment, the current taking it, and then the river absorbed it how the St. Lawrence absorbed everything that was put in it: completely, without comment, with the deep indifference of something that had been here before the city and would be here after it.

Renard watched it go.

Then he walked off the quay and into the city and Antoine watched him go and thought about the log in the river and thought about Blanchard's notebook and thought about the Governor's office and the machinery of administration and the ease with which things went where inconvenient truths went, and he thought about the city at the straits where none of this had happened yet, where the only record was the one in the ledger in the trunk on the quay, and he straightened his coat.

He picked up his commission papers.

He had been holding them under his arm since the gangplank and he took them out now and straightened them against his chest, the leather case solid and real and correctly worn at the corners, and he put them back inside his coat against his ribs where he could feel them. The authorization, the future, the thing that everything had been for.

He felt them against his chest.

He breathed.

He looked at the quay. At the passengers dispersing into the city, the ones who were going somewhere and the ones who were standing and not yet ready to go anywhere. At Beaumont, moving back toward him with the expression of a man who has more questions than answers, and had decided to start with the questions. At the soldiers on the deck of the ship above, their voices still carrying, working through whatever they were working through up there.

At the trunk on the quay stone.

At Marguerite beside him.

He walked away from the dock.

The two hired men took up the trunk.

They lifted it between them with the same careful-not-careful handling as before and settled it on their shoulders and followed Antoine off the quay; the trunk swaying slightly with the rhythm of their steps; the brass clasp catching the morning light at intervals as they walked, a small repetitive flash, there and gone, there and gone.

The quay fell behind them.

The city rose around them. The streets and the buildings and the sound of it, the sound of a city going about its morning, the horses and the voices and the smell of bread and wood smoke and the river, and Antoine walked through it with his commission against his ribs and a child's hand in his and the trunk on two men's shoulders behind him, and the city received him in the way cities receive men who arrive in them, which was without ceremony and without recognition and with the complete indifference of a place that has its own concerns.

He thought about Detroit.

He thought about the straits and the fort and the settlement and the future that had his name on it, the name that his grandmother's letter had told him would carry the shadow, the name that history would not treat simply, the name that was going to be synonymous with misfortune even as it built the thing that would outlast the misfortune. If he renounced his name.

He thought about this clearly and without the shadow's weight, similar to when you think about weather that you have been told is coming and that has not yet arrived, acknowledging it, accounting for it, continuing.

Marguerite walked beside him.

Her hand in his.

Her face forward.

Behind them, on the ship, the soldiers had come to the deck.

They stood at the gangplank's top and they looked at the deck in horror and they said the things that men said when they were looking at the indescribable, the urgent overlapping things, and the officer was among them and the officer was looking at the deck with the expression of a man who had been an officer for eleven years and had managed many situations and had arrived at a situation for which his eleven years had not prepared him. Vomiting occurred among the various soldiers, while some dropped their weapons and disembarked under duress.

He looked at the faces in the wood.

They looked up at him, and in their eyes was the silent agony of moans that could not be fully voiced.

He put his hand on the gangplank rail and he steadied himself and he breathed and he looked at the faces in the wood of the deck of La Vigilante and he thought about the report he was going to have to write and he thought about the report he was actually going to write, which would be different from the first report, because some things did not survive being written down in the way that formal reports were written down, they required a different kind of record, Blanchard's kind, the careful private kind, or they required no record at all, the Renard kind, the river kind.

He looked at the faces.

They looked up at the sky with their various expressions of the enormous.

He turned and went down the gangplank.

The fog continued to thin.

By midmorning the fog would be gone entirely, the St. Lawrence clear and bright under the autumn sun, the harbor busy with the ordinary traffic of a river port, the vessels and the workers and the trade and the life of a city going about the business of being a city.

La Vigilante would sit at the quay through the morning and the afternoon, and the evening. The officials would come and go. The reports would be filed, and the reports that needed to go elsewhere would go there. The passengers would be housed and documented and processed through the machinery of colonial administration. The soldiers would stand at the gangplank and not entirely understand what they were guarding or from what. Carpenters would be commissioned to attempt to remove the embedded humans within the ship.

At some point, later that day, or the next, or the one after — someone in authority would come to the quay with the intention of moving the ship to one of the massive lakes. Someone would board it and stand at the helm and find the helm turning on its own or not turning at all and they would get off the ship and there would be more reports and more machinery and eventually the ship would be scuttled or if possible salvaged. Her voyage would be removed from the royal ledger. Her official status, listed as lost at sea. And the faces in the wood — faces he knew they would not be able to remove. Those men would be fated to the bottom of the sea as well.

All of which would not be for a long time.

The river moved around the ship and the morning moved over the city and somewhere in the streets above the harbor Antoine de la Mothe Cadillac was walking toward the Governor's office with his commission against his ribs and a child beside him and a trunk behind him, and the trunk swayed with the rhythm of two men's steps, and inside it the ledger held its names, and the brass clasp caught the light at intervals as the hired men walked, there and gone, there and gone.

Patient.

Already thinking about Detroit.

Already thinking of the names of soldiers, harbormaster and a host of others who had witnessed this disembodiment.

Family names that he would give the demon that it might continue to prop up the name: Cadillac.

Antoine knew that between now and the expedition to find a fort encampment for his new city, there were a host of names he would have to add to the ledger.

History would blend into myth as stories of misfortune would settle over the land. Stories from families that would one day mention a red figure with glass for teeth looking at them as their fortunes turned to ash in their mouths.

An entity they would call the Nain Rouge.

To be continued...

Chapter Twenty-Two

Thank You

Thank you for sharing in the first book of this new supernatural horror series with me. More books are coming and I hope you will continue to follow my journey. You can be notified of new releases, giveaways and pre-release specials at http://donovanmneal.com

If you loved the book and would like to be informed of other books, please make sure you sign up to my mailing list here.

Lastly, feel free to leave a review! Your help in spreading the word is gratefully appreciated and reviews make a huge difference in helping new readers find the series.

God bless you and I hope to see you within the pages of the next book!

Remember...there will be more stories so sign up for the mailing list!

If you like adventure and fantasy check out Hutari.https://mybook.to/OpBRH

If you enjoy Christian speculative fiction check out the Third Heaven Series.https://mybook.to/iWRdO29

Chapter Twenty-Three

About the Author

Donovan M. Neal is the Amazon best-selling independently published author of the Third Heaven Series: a speculative Christian fantasy four book series that explores the captivating story about the fall of Lucifer. The book takes readers on an epic journey through the celestial realms, offering a unique perspective on the events surrounding Lucifer's rebellion and his descent into darkness.

In this imaginative tale, Donovan weaves together elements of Christian theology, angelic mythology, and fantastical world-building. The story delves into the cosmic conflict between good and evil, painting a vivid picture of the spiritual warfare that unfolded in the heavens.

Donovan has published fifteen books. His books have reached thirteen countries including India, Japan, the Philippines, Mexico, Brazil and across Europe, Canada and the US. He has sold over thirty thousand units of his books and generated over a quarter million in gross sales part time and without an agent. Donovan has produced fiction; non-fiction and most recently published a graphic novel. His genre of preference is fantasy and he has been named among such notable authors as Frank Perretti, Brian Godawa, and the late Dr. Michael S. Heiser.

When he's not writing or working, Donovan can be found gaming or enjoying various forms of media. He holds an undergraduate degree from the University of Michigan (Ann Arbor) and a graduate degree in Non-profit Management from Walden University. Prior to his current career, Donovan served in ordained ministry from 1993-2011 and has extensive experience teaching the Bible.

His favorite movie is the Lord of the Rings Trilogy. He also enjoys gaming and can be found on the PlayStation 5 deep in Destiny 2, He's owned most gaming systems all the way back from Atari and Pong! and has made several friends from his beloved days on World of Warcraft. A lover of such classics as chess and backgammon he loves most games and the strategy behind them.

When he is not imagining comic conflicts between good and evil he is helping to secure employment for housing insecure women as the Executive Director of a non-profit in the city of Detroit and also serves in the prayer and discipleship ministry of his local church.

www.ingramcontent.com/pod-product-compliance
Lightning Source LLC
LaVergne TN
LVHW041250110826
845146LV00005BA/1334

* 9 7 9 8 9 8 9 0 8 2 1 3 1 *